JESSICA BECK

CAST IRON WILL

THE CAST IRON COOKING MYSTERIES

The First Time Ever Published!

The First Cast Iron Cooking Mystery.

Introducing CAST IRON WILL, Book 1 in the brand new cozy mystery series, the Cast Iron Cooking Mysteries, from New York Times Bestselling Author Jessica Beck!

To P, for gleefully joining me on this
roller coaster ride called life!

When a customer is murdered on the front porch of the Cast Iron Store and Grill with one of their favorite skillets, fraternal twins Pat and Annie must solve the crime, or they just might be next items on the killer's to-do list.

CHAPTER 1: ANNIE

FINDING A BODY SLUMPED OVER in one of our rocking chairs on the Iron's front porch was just about the worst thing that had ever happened to me, and that counted losing my parents in a car wreck when my twin brother, Pat, and I were sixteen years old, more than a dozen years before. At first glance, I thought we simply had an early-morning visitor waiting for us to open the store and grill for the day, but the closer I got, the more I realized that whoever was perched there wasn't getting up again, at least not under their own power.

It was six thirty in the morning, and my day was suddenly getting off to a very bad start.

Not as bad as the person in that chair, though.

I didn't think things could get any worse, and then I saw a cast iron skillet, one of my favorite Griswolds, lying on the porch floor just behind the victim. From where I stood, I could see that there was something staining part of the iron, and I had a sick feeling that it was this poor soul's blood.

Somebody had used one of my favorite cooking instruments for murder.

Folks often ask me what it's like being a twin. Me, I wonder what it's like *not* being one. Sure, it can be comforting having someone so close to share just about everything with, especially growing up, but in the end, my brother and I are two different people, just like any other two siblings. We have a large number of similarities, but we have our differences, too. As for convenience, it's not like we can share clothes or anything. The truth is that my brother, Pat, would look ridiculous in one of my dresses, though I can normally be found at the Iron in blue jeans and a T-shirt.

The Iron. That's what we call the place we jointly own, formally known as The Cast Iron Store and Grill, which is a mouthful to say, particularly if you're in a hurry, which most folks seem to be in these days.

Our older sister, Kathleen, who just happens to be the sheriff in our little town of Maple Crest, North Carolina, says that my brother and I are equal parts weird/scary/odd the way we can communicate with each other without saying a word, but try sharing a womb with somebody for nine months and then get back to me. You can't get any closer than that. While Kathleen's out trying to keep the citizens of our little mountain town safe from the outside world—and each other, on occasion—Pat and I are keeping them fed, up to date, and well stocked with just about anything they need. The Iron is the lifeblood *and* the heartbeat of our little town. Nearly everyone in town comes by most days, either for my cooking—I specialize in food nearly always made in one of our cast iron skillets or pots—our general store where we sell a variety of the basic necessities and a few niceties, too, or the post office, where we deliver the mail. The latter is a small space that occupies one thin sidewall section of our building. After paying Edith Bost, a retired schoolteacher who's found a second career as our postmistress, to run the mail drop for us, we don't make a lot off of the arrangement, but it's a good way to keep our customers coming in.

We have a very specific division of labor at the Iron: I cook and run the grill, my brother oversees the cash register and the general store area, and Skip, our eighteen-year-old employee, helps out wherever we happen to need him at the time. If you'd ask him, though, he'd probably say that he's primarily there to run Skip's Corner, a small area on the sales floor that we've designated as his space to sell some of the crafts he loves making, from candles to soap to some of the funniest greeting cards anyone would ever want to send.

Between the four of us, we make a go of it, and somehow we manage to profit enough each month to stay afloat, no matter how troubling the times might be. It helps that Pat lives in the apartment above the store, so he doesn't have to pay anyone rent. Neither do I, for that matter. I live alone in my tiny home on the outskirts of town—a cabin perched on the edge of my very own lake—on eighty-five acres of land that's been in our family forever. I think Pat is crazy for living so close to where we work, and he thinks I'm equally insane being alone out in what essentially feels like the middle of nowhere to him.

I know that's a lot of information to swallow all in one gulp, but sometimes it's easier to get it all out there in the beginning, like speed dating, or how to sum up your life in thirty seconds or less.

———◆◇◆———

Now, back to the body. Before I called my older sister or even my twin, I had to see who had been murdered on the front porch of the Iron. Maybe they were even still alive, no matter how bad things looked from where I was standing. Who was it, anyway? Clearly a man: he was dressed in faded work pants, an old flannel shirt, and worn work boots, and he was sporting a battered old baseball cap with a tractor logo on the front of it. I couldn't even begin to guess how many men in our town that might describe, ranging from their early twenties to their late seventies. There was no other way around it; I was going to have to get a closer look.

As I knelt down and moved forward in order to check for a pulse and try to see the victim's face a little more clearly, my leg must have hit the chair's front rocker. Before I knew what was happening, the victim pitched forward out of the rocker and landed right on top of me, pinning me to the floor. As we both fell, his hat came off, and I could see that it was Chester Davis, one of our regular customers at the Iron. Who would want to kill Chester? As far as I knew, he was just a regular kind of guy in his late thirties, once divorced, a man I served breakfast to just about every morning. He'd always had a ready smile for me, and he never left a tip of less than twenty percent in our jar up front. I didn't have time to think much about motives at that moment, but it would certainly come to occupy my thoughts quite a bit later.

Right now, I had more immediate issues. What could I do with Chester's body pressing on me with a weight I had to struggle with to nudge even a little? I knew that it might have seemed as though I had a lot of time to think about my situation, but my thoughts were flying through my mind at the speed of light. Almost no time passed between Chester's tumble and my reaction to it.

In the end, I did what any sensible person in that situation would do.

I screamed.

CHAPTER 2: PAT

M Y TWIN SISTER, ANNIE, IS a great many things, but a screamer isn't one of them, so when I heard her yell just outside the front door of the Iron as I prepared to open the business for the day, I knew that I needed to come running, no questions asked.

I wasn't sure what I was expecting when I got out front, but finding her wrestling with one of our customers on the floor of the porch didn't even make the top one hundred on my list. "What's going on?" I asked her as I knelt down to lend a hand.

"Roll him off of me, Pat." I complied, grabbing the man's shoulder and flipping him over. It was Chester Davis, and his eyes were tightly shut when I saw his face.

"What happened? Did he faint?"

"Yeah, that's what happened. We were standing here having a nice little chat, and all of a sudden Chester pitched forward and pulled me down to the floor with him."

Annie could be sarcastic at times, particularly when she was scared. Or rushed. Or upset. Or impatient. Come to think of it, my twin had gotten a lot more of that particular trait than I had. As I finished dislodging Chester's body enough to free my twin, I helped her up and said, "Tell me what happened, Sis."

Annie took a deep breath, started to look down at Chester's body, and then she quickly looked away. "It was awful, Pat." Her voice sounded more like a little girl's than that of the woman she'd grown into.

I touched her shoulder lightly. "Take it easy. It's going to be okay."

"I don't see how." After a moment, she added, "I got out of my car and was heading up the stairs just like I do every day when I saw someone slumped over in one of our rocking chairs. Then I spotted my favorite skillet on the floor over there. It's got blood on it."

I glanced down at where she was pointing, and then I saw it myself. It had been partially hidden by Chester's leg when he'd fallen, but the pan was easy enough to make out after I knew where to look. Most of our friends had collected stamps, coins, even rocks when Annie and I had been kids, but we'd been hooked on cast iron even then. We didn't even have to buy it on occasion. Our local town dump had an area set up for residents to pick and choose from, and anything of value that the owner no longer wanted went there. Annie and I had marveled about the old cookware, brands like Wagner and Griswold and Montgomery Ward, and we'd quickly loaded up our wagon with the heavy ironware. On that first trip, we almost didn't make it home, it weighed so much. When we finally got there, we proudly showed our discoveries to our grandmother, who had loved cooking with cast iron since she'd been a girl, and that was when our obsession had started.

I took out my phone and dialed Kathleen's number. "We need to call Sis."

"That's a good idea." Annie was doing her best to keep her gaze averted from the scene, but I could tell by the tremor of her lower lip that she was close to losing it.

"Why don't you go inside and wait for her there?"

"Thanks, but I'm good right here," she replied. That was Annie, always strong, even when it cost her a little part of her soul.

"Kathleen, we need you at the Iron," I said when our older sister answered my call.

"What's wrong, did raccoons get into your storeroom again?" Our sister loved to tease us both, and she rarely missed an opportunity to chide us.

"I'm afraid that it's a little more grave than that. Somebody killed Chester Davis on our front porch." I hated the brutal way that it must have sounded to her, but it was the easiest way to convey the seriousness of the situation to her.

"What are you talking about, Pat? What happened? Tell me everything." There was a slight pause, and then she added, "On second thought, I'm two minutes away. Don't touch anything until I get there."

"Sorry, but it's too late for that," I said, but the phone was dead in my hand.

I'd tell her soon enough that we'd already disturbed the body.

While we waited, I grabbed my twin's hand to offer her what little comfort I could. "Kathleen's on her way."

Annie just nodded, clearly fighting back the tears.

Our elder sister was as good as her word, and in less than two minutes, she sped up to the Iron. At least she'd left her flashing lights and siren off. I had the feeling that we'd be getting plenty of attention because of the murder, and I wasn't in any hurry to get that started.

Kathleen jumped out of her squad car and raced to Chester's body. As she rushed toward him, she asked, "Did you two touch anything?"

"I turned him over," I admitted.

"Pat, you shouldn't have done that." Her words sounded ominous, as though I'd broken a law that I hadn't been aware of.

"He had to," Annie said softly.

"Why is that?" Kathleen asked as she searched in vain for a pulse.

"Mostly because Chester was on top of me."

Kathleen looked up at Annie, and then she stared hard at me. "Maybe you'd better start from the beginning."

7

After I gave her a brief summary of what had happened, Annie began to add something of her own to the conversation, but our older sister held up one hand impatiently as she asked, "We'll talk about it again later. For now, why don't you two wait inside? I'll be with you shortly."

"Can we make it quick? We open the store in ten minutes," I said as I glanced at my watch.

"Not today you don't. This entire place is a crime scene until I release it." Our sibling didn't leave any room for discussion, and I knew that it would be senseless to fight her on it. Besides, the last thing I wanted to do was to wait on customers after what had just happened. Maybe this time, I needed to just give in.

Annie and I went inside, and then we both headed straight for the front window where we could see what was going on. Kathleen was on her walkie-talkie, no doubt calling in her two employees on the force, Hank Timberline and Ginny Bost. Hank was nearing retirement age, while Ginny was barely out of the academy. I had to wonder what good either one of them would do Kathleen, but she hadn't asked me for my opinion, so I'd decided to keep it to myself. They arrived together a few minutes later, riding side by side in the town's only other squad car, stopping short and blocking our driveway to keep our customers out.

As they approached the Iron on foot, I asked my twin, "Would you like a cup of tea?"

"Do you have anything stronger upstairs?"

It was an odd request for her to make, since neither one of us drank, aside from a glass of wine with dinner every now and then. "I might have a root beer left in the fridge, but that's about it."

"Tea's fine," she said. "But I'll make it myself."

"I don't mind."

"Pat, I appreciate that, but it's still my grill," Annie said as she headed to the rear of the store, where her workstation was

8

located. There were no tables in our dining area, just a dozen round stools that spun around with a little effort at the extended bar. I took a seat on one of them and watched my twin fill a teapot and turn on one of the gas burners. "Would you like some, too?"

"Sure, why not?"

"I can't think of a reason in the world," she admitted.

We'd just finished our tea when the front door opened, and Kathleen walked in, a grim expression on her face. In her latex-gloved hand, she held the skillet in the air as she approached us. "Please tell me this doesn't belong to you."

CHAPTER 3: ANNIE

"I WOULD IF I COULD," I said, "but you know how much I hate lying to you. As a matter of fact, it happens to be my favorite skillet. I'm never getting it back, am I?" Why had I said that? A man was dead, and I was suddenly concerned about getting my favorite skillet back? I clearly wasn't myself. "I'm sorry. I didn't mean it that way."

Pat reached over and patted my arm. It was amazing how much just a tiny bit of contact from my twin eased my mind. He'd always had a calming effect on me, and I'd never needed it more than I did at the moment. I patted his hand absently in return as he said, "It's okay, Annie."

"I only wish that were true," Kathleen said as she placed the skillet in a brown evidence bag. "Based on my preliminary investigation, it's the murder weapon, so I'm not sure if you ever will get it back. Now, from the beginning, tell me what happened from the moment you found Chester's body."

I took a deep breath, and then I started to speak. "I was coming up the front steps and noticed Chester slumped over in one of our rocking chairs, though I didn't realize that it was him at that point. I didn't see the skillet right away, so I wondered if he was just napping. Then, when I saw the blood, I knew that he was in trouble. I knelt down and leaned forward so I could check for a pulse, and my leg must have hit the rocking chair leg. It moved enough to unseat Chester, and before I knew what was happening, I was pinned to the floor by a dead man."

"I heard her calling out, and a few seconds later I moved Chester's body just enough so that I could help Annie to her feet. The next thing we did was to call you," Pat explained, calmly and rationally. I had always been more inclined to let my emotions rule me, whereas my twin was the more cerebral of the two of us. Both parts came in handy at times, and right now, I wouldn't want Pat to be any other way.

"And neither one of you touched the skillet? Is that correct?"

"Not this morning, anyway," I said, and Pat echoed the fact that he hadn't handled it, either.

"Good," Kathleen replied, seeming happy with our admissions.

"But I touch that pan every day, so unless someone wiped it down after they walloped Chester with it, my fingerprints are bound to be all over it," I said. "Whenever I'm finished using any of my cast iron, I clean them, warm them up, and then I wipe them down with a very light coating of olive oil before I put them away. I can't help touching them all through the process."

"That's fine," Kathleen said absently.

"How is that fine?" Pat asked heatedly, certainly out of character from his normal calm demeanor. "Annie just admitted that her fingerprints are probably going to be all over a murder weapon. In what way possible could that be considered fine?"

"Take it easy, bro," I told Pat, trying to calm him down. My twin rarely raised his voice, no matter what the circumstances, so I knew that he was as rattled as I was about discovering Chester's body. "Let Kathleen do her job."

"Thanks," she said with a soft smile. "I've got more bad news for you. I'm afraid that you're going to be closed for the day. Could you call Skip and Edith and tell them not to bother coming in?"

"She's not going to like not being able to hand out the mail," I said. Edith was a widow well into her sixties, and despite that fact, she still somehow had more energy than Pat and me combined.

"I don't know what I can do about that," our older sister said with a frown.

Pat spoke up. "Why can't we open the back door and let folks come in that way? Chester never made it off the porch. Is there any reason you need to shut the *entire* Iron down?"

"Do you honestly feel like opening after what just happened?" Kathleen asked us both somberly.

"I know that it must sound counterintuitive to you, but it just might be the optimal thing we can do," I said. "After all, I've got a feeling that keeping busy is the only thing that is going to keep my mind occupied. If I'm busy cooking, I might not have as much time to think about Chester." I turned to Pat. "What do you say?"

"I'm okay with it if you are."

I turned to our sister. "Kathleen? Can we open?"

She frowned for a few moments before she spoke. "The truth is that I think you've both lost your minds, but you make a good point, Annie. Fine. Keep the front door bolted and the shades drawn, and you can go ahead and open for business, as long as it doesn't interfere with official police business."

"Thank you," I said, and then I hugged her. Kathleen usually shied away from public displays of affection while she was in uniform, but I was glad that she was making an exception for me. It probably didn't hurt that the three of us were the only ones there.

"You're welcome. Just don't let anyone out the front door, and we should be okay," she instructed.

"We won't."

After Kathleen was gone, Pat and I walked to the front of the store, dead bolted the door, and then we pulled every shade that faced the front porch until that part of the building's interior was cast in shadows. Pat turned and looked at me for a moment before he spoke. "Sis, are you sure about this?"

"No, but it's the best option we have, don't you think?"

"I suppose so. Honestly, the only way we'll probably be able to cope with Chester's murder right now is to try to act as though nothing happened."

"I don't want to do that," I said out loud as a thought that had been growing in my mind was starting to demand to go public.

"No, of course not," Pat backpedaled. "I don't want to ever forget about what happened to Chester, either. Maybe we should have a memorial or something for him."

"That's not what I was talking about," I said. "Pat, I think you and I should try to figure out who killed the man ourselves."

CHAPTER 4: PAT

"**Y**OU WHAT? YOU CAN'T BE serious." My twin sister had had some crazy ideas in the past, but this one trumped them all. "Annie, we're not even the least bit qualified to solve a murder."

"What have we been reading since we could hold books?" she asked me. "Mysteries! We cut our teeth on the Hardy Boys and Nancy Drew, and we've kept the habit all the way through to the latest cozy trends."

"I can't argue with the fact that between the two of us, we've read more mysteries than anyone else in this part of the state," I admitted. "But solving a fictional case is a lot easier than doing it in real life."

"You've heard Kathleen. Most crooks aren't exactly rocket scientists. We're bound to be smarter than they are."

"Why not let our big sister do her job, and we'll do ours?"

"Because this is personal," Annie answered grimly. "Chester was murdered on our front porch with my favorite skillet. How much more involved can we be?"

"You've got a point there," I conceded, "but I still think it's dangerous."

"What have we always said, Pat? There's nothing that the two of us can't accomplish if we put our minds together. Why should this be any different?"

"I can guarantee you that Kathleen's not going to like it one little bit."

Annie frowned. "Probably not. We'll have to keep what we're doing from her until we're ready to give her the killer's name."

"Do you honestly think that it's going to be as easy as all that?"

"Pat, we both know that Kathleen is a fine sheriff, but how many real murders has she ever had to investigate during her tenure? I'm not talking about the few cases of drunken homicide she's had to deal with, or any of the other run-of-the-mill murders that have happened on her watch. I'm talking about cases that require a special skill set for investigation. Think about it. Folks around here are cautious about what they say to her when she's asking questions as the sheriff, but they all talk to us freely. Plus, between the two of us, we know everyone in Maple Crest. Not only that, but we know what buttons we need to push to get answers, and if someone's acting out of character, we'll realize it before anyone else does. Come on, Pat. This is important."

"I couldn't agree with you more," I said, "but just because we can do something doesn't mean that we should."

Annie took a deep breath, and then, in a voice I recognized as being as serious as she could get, Annie said, "Patrick, his body was right on top of me. Someone obviously has a grudge against us, and if we don't catch them, one of us might be next."

Annie rarely used my full given name, just as I didn't call her Analeigh unless the circumstances were particularly dire. Still, her conclusion was a little hard to swallow. "What makes you think the killer didn't just take advantage of the opportunity to kill Chester when he was alone? It could just be a coincidence that it happened on our porch."

"Maybe so, but how do you explain my skillet being used as a murder weapon? Whoever did it had to have at least planned that part of it out."

Annie had a point, and I felt myself coming around to my twin's point of view. "So answer me this. What do we have in common with Chester Davis that might make someone come after us, too?"

My twin's look of delight warmed my heart. "Does that mean that we're going to do it?"

"It appears that it would at least be prudent to look into this a little further," I said, trying not to encourage her too much. When my sister's enthusiasm was on fire, it was difficult not getting swept up by the oncoming flames.

Trying her best to look somber, Annie nodded. "Prudent. That's the perfect way to put it."

"So, where should we get started?" I asked her.

"First off, we need to make a list. Don't our favorite authors all do that?"

I nodded as I reached behind the counter and pulled out a plain brown paper bag after I grabbed one of the pens from the register. When I looked up at Annie, I was faced with a look of disappointment on her face. "What's wrong? Don't you want to write things down?"

"Why don't we use the menu board instead?" she suggested, pointing to the big whiteboard near the grill in back where she wrote her daily specials.

"Because we don't want the world to see what we're up to. Honestly, we probably don't even want Skip or Edith to know."

"Why shouldn't we recruit them to help us with our cause?" Annie asked.

"Can you really see either one of them keeping it a secret?"

She frowned before she spoke. "Point taken. It's got to just be the two of us, then."

"Well, we've always been up for any challenge in the past," I said, "though this is bound to be the hardest thing we've ever faced."

"I know that, but don't forget, we have another advantage over Kathleen."

"What's that? She's a trained law enforcement officer with

years of experience on the job. What can we possibly bring to the table that our sister can't?"

"We have twin power," Annie said with a grin.

As kids, we'd made up our own superhero characters—twins, naturally enough—that solved crimes and saved the world on a daily basis. "Do you think that's going to help us in real life?"

"Why shouldn't it?"

I shrugged. "There are so many reasons, I can't even begin to count them." I tore the bag down one side and spread the paper out into a single layer. "Now, before our staff arrives, let's make a list of everyone we know who might have wanted to see Chester Davis dead."

"That might prove to be difficult," Annie said. "I can't imagine anyone openly hating him, can you?"

"He was a good guy, but I'm sure that he had enemies like everyone else, though I can't imagine anyone hating him enough to murder him in premeditation."

"Should we explore motives first, then?" Annie asked me. "That might tell us why someone would kill him, and then we could look for folks who matched the rationale."

"We might as well try it. After all, nobody's going to ever know what we're doing but us, if we do it correctly." I started writing, explaining as I went. "Off the top of my head, rationales for murder that I can come up with are greed, lust, love, revenge, protecting a secret, stopping someone from doing something, defending someone from the victim, or just plain, old-fashioned hate. Do you have anything to add to my list?"

Annie whistled softly. "Wow, you rattled off that list pretty quickly. Do you spend a lot of time thinking about motives for murder, Pat?"

"Only when things are slow in my part of the Iron," I said with a grin.

"Remind me never to cross you, Brother."

"You, of all the people in the world, have nothing to worry about from me. After all, killing you would feel too much like suicide." I hoped that my grin conveyed the fact that I was just teasing her. I couldn't imagine my life without my twin sister, and if anything ever happened to her, I wasn't sure that I would be able to go on.

"Again, good to know," she answered, smiling back. "I think you've covered all of the bases for now, unless something comes up later."

"Fine. The next question is, who do we know that fits into any of these categories?"

My sister was about to answer when the back door opened. Fearing that it was Kathleen, I haphazardly folded the bag back together and buried it under the others.

It wasn't our sister, though.

Our two employees were coming into work, chattering about what they'd just seen outside. It was going to be difficult keeping our investigation from them, but I'd meant what I'd told Annie. While it was true that Skip and Edith might be able to bring new information to the table, there was no way that either one of them would be able to keep the fact that we were digging into murder a secret, and that was one of the main things that Annie and I had going for us. If the killer didn't even suspect that we were investigating the crime, they might just slip up and tell us something by accident. The fact that we didn't want Kathleen to find out what we were doing was a factor as well, but I decided not to dwell on that. If she ever did discover what we were up to before we handed the killer to her wrapped up neatly in a pretty bow, I couldn't imagine the wrath my twin and I would face.

CHAPTER 5: ANNIE

"**G**OOD MORNING**," I SAID AS I gave Pat a warning look not to say anything to Skip or Edith. I loved my twin brother more than I could ever express, but sometimes he had difficulty knowing when to talk and when to keep his yap shut. "Thanks for coming in today. Listen, given what just happened, if either one of you would rather forget about work today, it's perfectly understandable."

"My dear, sweet child," Edith said as she approached me with a concerned "mother hen" expression on her face. "Are you all right?" Though she was getting on in years, Edith normally exuded a youthful zest for life that sometimes put mine to shame, though something was different about her demeanor now; apparently murder brought out the nurturer in her. Edith was a petite woman, her figure no doubt just as trim as it had been when she'd been a teenager, and while most women her age seemed to go for a multitude of hair dyes, frostings, and even wigs, Edith proudly sported her own natural silver-gray hair, cut short in a stylish bob.

As she took a few steps toward me, I had to stop her before she tried to hug me. "I didn't actually see the killer," I admitted. "You know that, right?"

"I understand, but finding poor Chester like that must have been absolutely traumatic for you."

"I have to admit, it wasn't the highlight of my day," I admitted, "but I'm okay now. I feel bad for Chester, though."

"I can't believe we had a murder right here at the Iron," Skip said, a little too excitedly for my taste. He'd just turned eighteen, but while a great many of his contemporaries were heading off to college, the armed forces, or even matrimony, our Skip had a single-minded passion for one thing. Besides his love of crafting, he was convinced that he was the next great entrepreneur-inventor, always searching for the one perfect idea that would skyrocket him to fortune, though not necessarily fame. Skip was tall and skinny, and he sported a mop of chestnut hair that was constantly in need of a trim, but when it came to hard work, he was never afraid of getting his hands dirty. "I didn't think anything happened in Maple Crest."

"I would have just as soon have had it happen somewhere else," I said. "So, what do you two say? Would you like to skip out today with no hard feelings?"

Edith frowned before she spoke. "If it's all the same to you and Pat, I'd rather be here manning my station. After all, I took an oath." If she'd recited any words of honor and duty about working at our dinky little satellite post office, I hadn't heard about it, but then again, Edith always had considered her job more of a calling than an occupation.

"Skip? How about you?"

"I'm good," he said as he glanced at the big clock mounted over the front door. "How are we going to tell folks that we're here, though? When I rode in on my motorcycle, I had trouble getting in. The police had the driveway blocked."

"I had to park down the block in front of Murphy's," Edith echoed, naming the only real furniture store we had in town. "Let me tell you, Betty Murphy looked none too pleased about me taking one of her parking spaces. She acts as though she owns the street itself."

"I'll see what I can do," I said. "Pat? Do you want to get things ready in here while I go talk to Kathleen?"

"Maybe I should be the one to speak with her," my twin

volunteered. "I'm sure you have work to do to get ready for your grill customers."

I knew why my brother was offering to speak with our older sister. He didn't quite trust me to be diplomatic when I asked her to kindly get her squad cars out of our customers' way. Where he got the notion that I couldn't be as cordial and sweet as the next person was beyond me. "Thanks for offering, but I don't mind doing it. Until we find a way to get our customers into the Iron, I don't have anything to do, anyway."

"I could make a sign," Skip offered.

"You do that," I said as I winked at Pat.

He understood by my grin that I wasn't going to budge, and bless his heart, he knew better than to try to fight me. After all, I was the older of the two of us, even if it was just by seven minutes, a fact that I rarely gave him the opportunity to forget. In my mind, he was the baby of the family, a title that he didn't have to share with anyone else, particularly me. "Remember, you need to be civil," he told me sternly.

"Me? I'll be the very picture of Southern grace and charm."

That made him laugh, which was my goal. I decided to walk out on that note and go in search of our older sister.

I didn't have far to go.

Apparently she was on her way into the Iron to have a word with us, and from the expression on her face, I knew that it wasn't going to be good.

———◦◇◦———

"Annie, we've got a problem," Kathleen said as we approached each other just outside the back door. There were woods both beside and behind the Iron, something that I thought made the place feel as though it had been set down rather than been built in place.

"I'd think that we had more than one," I admitted. "Are you

talking about Chester's murder, or is there something else that's happened that I don't know about?"

"Grady Simpson just left," she said, and I didn't need any further explanation than that. Grady ran the town's pennysaver, a combination gossip sheet/newspaper/swap meet/flea market of a paper that rarely had any news deeper than who was spotted leaving town in the middle of the night or what prominent member of our council was known to take a sip or three too many of red wine sitting on her porch after work most nights. Grady was, plain and simple, a gossip hound. How women ever got the reputation for spreading stories was beyond me. When it came to Maple Crest gossip, Grady was king, queen, and every member of the royal court all wrapped up into one.

"Why am I not surprised? You had to know that he'd hear about the murder sooner or later, Kathleen."

My older sister frowned. "I told you to call me Sheriff when I'm working in my official capacity. I was willing to let it slide earlier because of what you'd been through, but it's important to me that you do it now, okay?"

I looked around to see who might be listening to us standing on the back porch, but if anyone was there, I couldn't see them. Still, I understood her desire to keep her family life and her work status separate, so I decided to do my best to comply. After all, if she found out what Pat and I were about to do, I'd need every last bit of goodwill from her that I could muster.

"Sorry," I said as contritely as I could manage without sounding sarcastic. "Pat and I were wondering if you wouldn't mind moving your cars so our customers can drive up and park in our lot."

"You're not upset about Grady? He's going to slander you up one side and down the other. You know that, don't you?"

"Isn't it libel when he does it in print?" I asked her with a grin.

Kathleen snorted. "Of course it is, but you're missing my point."

"Sheriff," I said carefully, "worrying about Grady Simpson is about the least productive thing in the world that I could do with my time. He's going to say what he's going to say, and folks are either going to take it all with a huge pinch of salt, or they'll be inclined to believe him. Either way, I don't see how it's my problem."

"Not until it impacts your business, anyway," she said seriously.

"I appreciate you worrying about us, but right now, the only thing that's slowing up our business are the two police cruisers sitting out front."

"We'll move them over to the side lot in a second," she reluctantly agreed, "but I'm not sure how you're ever going to get your customers to come inside. Most folks are going to want to have themselves more than a little peek at what we're doing, though they won't have Chester to look at for much longer. We've taken all of the video and the photographs that we need, and Doc Blackberry is already on his way." Our one town GP, Doctor Jacob Blackberry, was a jack of all trades, delivering babies, holding general office hours, and working as the town coroner. I didn't know how he managed to get by, but he loved small-town life, and we knew that we were lucky to have him.

"Just let me know when we can have the front porch back," I said.

For a moment, my sister's hard exterior softened a bit. "Annie, are you really as okay as you're acting?"

"That depends. Is it the sheriff asking me, or is it my older sister?"

She smiled ruefully at me. "For one second, let's assume that it's your sister."

"Honestly, I'm probably still in shock," I admitted. "I may need to call you later and talk." My sister was an excellent listener, and while I usually discussed everything going on in my life with Pat, there had been some things growing up that I wasn't going to share with any boy, even if we had occupied the same egg once upon a time.

"Day or night, Analeigh, I'm there for you," she said, her voice still soft.

"I know that, and I appreciate it," I answered as Skip came out carrying a sign nicely printed on a sheet of white cardboard and attached to a wooden stake.

"How's this look?" he asked me.

I read the words aloud. "'Yes, we're open. Come in around back.' I like it. I've got to say, your printing is a lot better than mine."

"When you make as many homemade greeting cards as I do, you get pretty good at it over time," he said proudly. "Where should I put it?"

"Come on," Kathleen said. "I'll show you as soon as we move our cars."

"Thanks," I said with a smile.

"You're welcome. I still think that you and your brother are crazy for opening the store after what just happened, but you've both always been a little odd to me."

"To you and the rest of the world," I replied. I glanced over my sister's shoulder and saw an ambulance pulling up in front. "Is that really necessary?"

"We can't exactly haul the victim off in the back of a pickup truck," Kathleen said. "Don't worry. You should have your porch back around four."

"Perfect. That's just in time for us to close the place for the day," I said, this time letting a bit of my frustration through.

"What can I say? These things take time. Just be glad you're getting it back at all. Talk to you later, Annie."

As Skip and Kathleen headed toward the front of the building, I decided that it was time to go back inside and get the grill ready to serve breakfast, just in case any of our customers dared step inside after what had happened to poor Chester.

***

I loved having my very own fancy range/griddle/oven combo in my little space near the back of the store. The entire unit ran on natural gas, so even when our power was out because of snow or even heavy rain, I could still feed the masses when they came by the Iron for a meal. The range sported six burners, a twenty-four-inch griddle, and two standard ovens, everything I needed to cook except a fire pit, but there were no worries there, either; I had one of those out back, where I taught rustic cast iron cooking classes four times a year. The best thing of all was that the entire operation was just five feet wide and three feet deep, a real economy given the cramped space I had to work in. All in all, my little setup took up minimal floor space, including the seating and the bar. It might have been a small part of the Iron, but it was all mine.

Menus were simple enough. For breakfast, I offered waffles, pancakes, biscuits, bacon, sausage, and of course, the basic egg, served all the way from scrambled to fried. There were omelets on the menu occasionally, stuffed with peppers, onions, ham, and cheese, but those were offered only now and then. I liked to keep my morning fare plain and predictable. Lunch could be anything I felt like making in my cast iron, from stews to chicken to ribs, with cornbread, more biscuits, and even dessert prepared in the dense black metal. For those with more pedestrian tastes, I also served up hamburgers, hot dogs, and grilled cheese sandwiches, something that never changed. I liked serving breakfast and lunch, leaving dinner for others to prepare and serve. The grill suited me, and I was at my happiest wielding a spatula or one of my precious cast iron pots or pans.

I whipped up some biscuit dough as the left oven preheated. The griddle surface was as smooth and as slick as a mirror, and why shouldn't it be? I spent every afternoon honing it with a pumice stone, making sure that it was pristine before I left for the day. I loved my old cast iron, particularly my Griswolds and Wagners, cast from a different generation, not that there wasn't room for the occasional Lodge in my armory of cookware. No matter what year it was made, cast iron was my favorite way to cook, and I used it whenever the opportunity presented itself, which was for just about anything in the spectrum with two notable exceptions: I wouldn't fry eggs in my iron cookware, and I wouldn't use tomatoes in most forms. As far as I was concerned, the acid cut straight through the seasoning, which was a thin coating of carbonized oil that built up over the years on the pans and made them all virtually nonstick surfaces.

Cast iron was my profession as well as my hobby, but trivets were my indulgence. First created to hold hot skillets and pots, they were also beautiful in their own right, in my opinion, and always hanging within reach, I had mostly Griswold editions featuring stained glass patterns, eagles in wreaths, ornately designed trees, stars, intricate circular patterns, and more. Their delicate yet iron-tough characteristics really sang to me for some reason.

For eggs, I kept a few aluminum pans on hand, and for my tomato sauces and chilis, a couple of porcelain enameled cast iron pots worked wonderfully.

As I looked over my array of pots and pans, I was satisfied that I was ready to create any order that came my way.

Now all I needed was customers.

CHAPTER 6: PAT

I F SOMEONE FROM THE OUTSIDE happened to glance in through one of our windows, it probably looked like a typical day at the Iron. Annie was getting ready to serve breakfast, Edith was busy sorting the day's mail and shoving it into all of the quaint little boxes, Skip was restocking the batteries and pumpkin butter, and I was restocking the till with cash from our safe. I felt secure enough about the money we kept on hand at the shop, since the safe was embedded in concrete under the floor and was only accessible by a trapdoor behind the counter up front, where I spent most of my days. If someone wanted to break into it, they'd probably need a jackhammer to do it. I was just adding the singles to the appropriate slot in the register when I heard the back door open. We'd installed little bells on both the front and back entrances so we'd know when someone was coming in or going out when we'd first opened, and though it had taken a little time to get used to at first, it was music to my ears now.

I was even happier when I realized that it wasn't my sister, Kathleen, or one of her deputies.

It appeared that we had an actual customer, our first of the day.

———◆⬥◆———

It was Bryson Oak. He stopped at Annie's station, so I figured he must be having his typical breakfast, but he surprised me by not lingering there for very long before he walked over to me. Somewhere in his late thirties, Bryson was short and heavyset as well as balding prematurely, not a generally attractive combination. Despite all of his physical limitations, Bryson considered himself a ladies' man, and to my constant surprise, he seemed to do quite well with the opposite sex. I had to wonder if it had more to do with his air of confidence than anything else, but somehow he'd found a way to make it work for him. Usually, at any rate. I knew from the town scuttlebutt that Bryson and Chester had been rivals, not friends, in business as well as in love, so I wondered what was bringing him to me the morning his nemesis was murdered on my front porch.

I didn't have long to wait until I found out.

"Pat, do you have a second?"

I closed the till before I answered him. "Sure thing, Bryson. What's up?"

He lowered his voice when he answered, though no one else was within earshot of us. "I just heard about Chester."

"News travels fast around here, doesn't it?" I asked noncommittally.

"Have you spoken with your sister?"

I looked at him oddly before I replied. "I talk to Annie just about every minute of every day that we're awake. Why?"

Bryson shook his head. "I'm not talking about that sister. I meant Kathleen."

"The sheriff? Yes, she and I have discussed what happened." What was he getting at? Was the man actually expecting me to disclose something to him that my sister might have shared with me in confidence? Kathleen wouldn't do that in the first place, and if she had, I wouldn't tell Bryson, and he should know better.

"What did she have to say?"

I wasn't going to answer his question, but it didn't keep me from making a query of my own. "Why the sudden concern? You two weren't exactly best friends when he was alive, were you?"

Bryson looked at me distastefully. "Just because we weren't drinking buddies doesn't mean that I don't care about what happened to him."

"Sorry, but I don't buy it," I said.

He looked stunned by my response. "Why not?"

"It's simple. You've never shown any interest in Chester one way or another unless it was a way to top him at something, so your sudden concern about what happened to him this morning doesn't ring true."

Bryson pursed his lips a moment or two before he spoke again. "I'm guessing you haven't heard, then, have you?"

"Heard what?"

"I've been dating Julia for the past three weeks," he finally admitted.

"Julia Crane?" I asked.

"She's the only Julia in town, as far as I know."

I whistled softly. "You don't say. How did you manage to keep that a secret? I figured if you were dating Chester's ex-wife, the whole town would know about it."

"As a matter of fact, I was fine with it being out in the open, but Julia didn't want Chester to find out," he replied sullenly.

"They've been divorced for over a year now. Why should what he thought matter to her in the least?" This was a curious conversation I was having with Bryson, but if he was going to share information about possible motives with me, I wasn't about to stop him.

"That's what I kept asking her."

"What did she say?" I asked, and then I noticed Annie heading over to us. If she joined our conversation, she might inhibit Bryson from saying anything else, so I shook my head so slightly that I doubted Bryson would pick up on it. It was a part of the "twin language" that Annie and I had developed early on. Some folks believed it was ESP, and I don't have any cause to doubt that it's a possibility in some twins under certain circumstances, but this was just a case of subtle signs that we'd spent a lifetime developing. Annie veered off at the last second and headed over toward Skip to lend him a hand in restocking the shelves. It was so subtle that I doubted that Bryson had even noticed. "Surely she had to give you some kind of reasonable answer."

"She said that he was still in love with her," Bryson admitted.

"Did she feel the same way about him?"

He gave me a brief glance full of contempt. "How could she? She was with me."

"That doesn't answer my question," I pressed.

"I just wanted to know if the sheriff had mentioned me, that's all."

"Your name never came up in our conversation," I replied. *Though it certainly will now*, I added, but only in my own head. Bryson was showing way too much interest in Chester's murder as far as I was concerned, and that only served to make me suspicious about his motivation. Was his confession of a relationship with the victim's ex-wife simply a way to get it out into the open before my older sister uncovered it? What other motive would he have had for sharing the news with me?

"Good. Let's keep it that way, okay?"

I wasn't about to honor that particular request. I glanced over at Annie, who was waiting for a sign from me that she could join us, and I figured that it was time. I barely winked at her, a flash of recognition that I doubted anything but a high-speed camera could pick up, and she was with us before I was forced to lie to Bryson about what I was planning on doing next.

Annie smiled brightly at our visitor. "How about that breakfast? I can have your usual whipped up in half a shake."

"Thanks, but I'm not all that hungry this morning after all," Bryson said.

"Come on, Bryson. Starving yourself isn't going to do Chester any good," Annie prodded good naturedly. "How about if I give you a discount, good today and today only?"

"I appreciate the sentiment, but like I said, I'm not interested."

Bryson headed out the door, and I doubted that he would have moved any faster if the place had been on fire.

"Annie, I've never heard you offer a discount on your food since we opened the Iron," I said to my sister after Bryson was gone.

"It's a first, but I wanted to see just how strong his urge to leave really was."

"He seemed pretty intent on getting away from us, didn't he?" I asked.

"What did he just tell you?" she asked earnestly. "And don't even think about leaving anything out. I want to know every word that he said."

"The gist of it was that Bryson's been dating Julia Crane for the last three weeks."

Annie looked suitably startled by the news. "Chester's ex? You're kidding."

"I don't know if it's true or not, but that's what he just told me," I said.

"What did Chester have to say about that?" Annie asked.

"As far as Bryson knew, he wasn't aware of it. It seems they were keeping it from him."

"That doesn't sound like Bryson Oak," Annie said. "I'm surprised he didn't take out a full-page ad in Grady's pennysaver newspaper. I wonder why they kept it so hush-hush."

"According to Bryson, Julia told him that Chester was still in love with her."

Annie frowned upon hearing the news before speaking

again. "That might explain things if I'd found Bryson's body out front this morning, but it doesn't help us figure out why Chester was murdered."

"Here are a pair of possibilities," I said off the top of my head. "Let's assume for one second that it's true that Chester still loved his ex-wife. What if he found out that Bryson was dating her, and he confronted his rival on the front porch? Things could have gotten ugly fast."

"Then again, it could have been Julia. Chester could have invited her here for breakfast to talk to her, and somehow it came out that she was dating Bryson. Chester could have reacted badly to the news about the relationship, he and Julia could have struggled, and he was murdered in the bargain."

I shook my head. "It won't work, because we're forgetting one very important fact."

"What's that?"

"Whoever killed Chester stole one of your skillets to use as a murder weapon. That means that it was premeditated, and also that whoever did it was trying to cast suspicion on us in the process."

"On me, you mean," Annie said.

"It could have just as easily have been meant for me," I said.

"Honestly, Pat, when's the last time you used a skillet to cook?"

"Hey, I might not use the Griswolds as much as you do, but I still know my way around the grill. After all, this place is called the Iron because we *both* love cast iron."

"You're right," Annie said contritely, apologizing immediately. My twin could really rattle my cage at times, but she also knew how to apologize with her entire heart. "I'm sorry. I didn't mean to exclude you. Until we know better, we need to assume that we were both targeted."

"Why does that admission not make me feel any better?" I asked her with a smile.

"Maybe because it involves both of us and not just one of us."

"If I have to have a target painted on my back, I'd just as soon have you watching out for me."

"Right back at you," Annie said lightly, and then she frowned. "You know, they were both here yesterday."

"Bryson and Julia?"

"Yes. I served them lunch, at different times, heck, even different meals, but one of them could have slipped out with the skillet when I wasn't watching."

"The skillet wouldn't exactly be easy to smuggle out without anyone noticing, would it?"

"You'd be surprised," Annie said. "It's a Griswold number 5, which puts it at approximately eight inches across and a little over two pounds. That's plenty of weight to be lethal if it were swung hard enough. The truth is, it wouldn't be hard at all to slip it under a jacket or even into an oversized bag like the one Julia was carrying yesterday."

"It still doesn't answer the question of why someone would try to drag us into it."

"We're going to have to be patient, Pat. If it were easy, everyone would be solving crimes, now, wouldn't they?"

I smiled slightly. "You've got a point." I looked around the empty space. "Do you think any of our customers will ever come back?"

"Once the word gets out, we're going to be crawling with people, just you wait and see."

"Do you honestly think so?"

"If I know the fine folks of Maple Crest, they're going to want to see where the murder occurred, and they'll be asking questions, too."

I shuddered a little. "That sounds a little ghoulish, don't you think?"

"Pat, whether we like it or not, it's the most excitement we've had in town since the football team stole the cannon on the town square on homecoming three years ago."

"I suppose that's true."

"Look at it this way. If they come by to gawk, they'll feel obligated to order food or at the very least to buy something. We didn't have anything to do with Chester's murder, so there's no reason to punish the Iron. Besides, if we keep our eyes and ears open, we might just uncover a new lead or two while we're working."

Annie had a point. She could be pragmatic when it suited her, but I'd meant what I'd said.

The sooner we solved this murder, the quicker we could get back to our lives, something I very much wanted to happen.

But it wasn't going to occur unless my twin sister and I did some serious digging, and fast.

CHAPTER 7: ANNIE

IT TURNED OUT THAT I was even more on the money than I'd imagined when I'd told Pat that our customers would be back. Within half an hour, the Iron was hopping with people, all curious about what had happened to Chester Davis. I overheard several theories espoused as I cooked, each wilder than the one before it, but I paid attention to each and every one of them. How could I know if one of my customers might just have gotten it right?

The grill itself was busy, with all twelve of my barstools occupied, and half a dozen other folks hovering nearby, browsing among Pat's shelves and picking up things to buy while they waited for a spot to open up. It often worked out that way when we were at our busiest, and some of our regulars fussed that they had to wait for a place at the bar, but we were happy with the system as it stood. After all, Pat wasn't all that keen on the space I was already taking up, let alone ready to allow me to put a few tables in, even though he knew that the food I offered served as a draw for the rest of the place.

It was busy, but I never felt any pressure, no matter how many diners I had waiting to be seated. Cooking on the range was fun as I danced among the six burners, two feet of griddle, and the pair of large ovens beneath them.

I worked in silence to music that only I could hear, flipping hash browns and pancakes on the griddle, plating fried eggs as I added a few slices of bacon I'd just finished cooking, and grabbing a few biscuits, all the while scraping the grill down for my next order. I'd tried hiring help one summer to serve the food for me, but we'd just ended up getting in each other's way. Over the years, I had mastered the art of taking orders, cooking them, and then turning one step back to serve them, sliding the bill under the plate just before it landed. At least I didn't have to worry about taking payments and making change; Pat handled all of that up front at his register. I'd argued that having a tip jar on the counter near me when the co-owner ran the grill was a little off-putting, but when my customers had insisted on leaving me tips tucked under their plates anyway, I'd installed a handy jar at the counter. There was a note on it that stated that all tips were donated to our local animal rescue center, and that seemed to appease everyone, with the added bonus of making me feel good every time someone slipped a single—or even a dime for that matter—into the jar.

As I worked, I continued to eavesdrop on my customers. It didn't bother me in the slightest, since none of them had any real expectation of privacy. After all, they had to figure that *someone* would be listening.

"Had you seen Chester lately?" Darrel Hodges asked Jimmy Oleander as they ate their breakfasts. Darrel was a sculptor in wood, and quite a good one, while Jimmy served as the town's chief maintenance engineer. That man could fix anything that had ever broken, and if Humpty Dumpty had gone to him for help, he'd have been whole again in no time.

"As a matter of fact, I talked with him the day before yesterday," Jimmy said as he mopped up some egg yolk with a piece of buttered biscuit with fingers constantly darkened by working on oily machines and never completely clean. I'd made sausage gravy earlier using a cast iron skillet and one of my gas burners, and Jimmy had requested extra gravy. I'd buried his biscuit in an avalanche of the stuff, bringing a smile to his face that I doubt anyone had seen in awhile. He often moonlighted after his regular working hours were over, and Pat and I had used his services a few times in the past when we'd needed something around the Iron fixed.

"How did he seem to you?" Darrel asked. The man was an artist with any carving tool imaginable, from a dental probe to a chainsaw, and I'd heard that some of his work was featured in some of the nicer homes across the country. You'd never know it by his demeanor, though. He was as humble as a bag of dirt, as he liked to say whenever he was given the chance.

"He was a little off, truth be told," Jimmy reported. "He kept mumbling about something that didn't make any sense to me when I was over there working at his place."

"What were you doing for him?" Darrel asked. It was the wrong question in my mind. I wanted to shout, "What did he say?" but if I did that, then they'd both know that I'd been listening in.

"He wanted me to reinforce the hinges on his safe," Jimmy said. "I told him that it couldn't be done. If he wanted something stronger than what he had, he was going to have to order it."

"I'll bet he didn't like that one little bit."

Jimmy shrugged. "It didn't take him long to see that I was right. While I was standing there, he got on the phone and ordered a safe that would withstand anything short of an atomic bomb going off nearby."

"What do you suppose he was going to keep in there?" Darrel asked.

Wow. That was a good question that it hadn't even occurred to me to ask. Maybe it was good that I couldn't just interrupt their flow.

"That's what he was mumbling about. He kept saying, 'They're mine, and nobody else's. Nobody's going to steal them from me. Nobody.'"

"That's kind of odd," Darrel replied. "I wonder what he didn't want stolen."

"Is that the first question that came into your head?" Jimmy asked as he sopped up more gravy. There wasn't much biscuit left, but that didn't stop him from shoveling the gravy into his mouth anyway. After he finished his bite, he said, "I kept wondering who he thought might be wanting to steal from him."

"That's a good question, too," Darrel said. He'd finished his breakfast, and I could see a few other patrons eyeing him as they frowned for his benefit. It was my policy that if folks were waiting, nobody got to dawdle, and I meant it. I'd been known to scare a customer away by slamming my spatula down on the counter in the past, but I couldn't bring myself to do it at the moment. I needed to give the two men time to finish their conversation.

I was thwarted in that as well, though, as Jimmy pushed his plate away and collected his bill. "Maybe we'd better finish this conversation outside. There's quite a line forming back there."

Darrel looked up, and he seemed surprised to see that Jimmy was telling the truth. He grabbed his own check, and then he snatched up Jimmy's. "I've got this one."

"You paid last time," the maintenance man protested.

"I know, but I just sold a piece to a guy in Seattle, and I want to celebrate. That's why I asked you to join me for breakfast."

Jimmy shook his head. "You call having a meal with me celebrating? Man, I don't think that word means what you think it does."

"Jimmy, we've been friends since we got put in opposite corners in first grade for cutting up during class. Who else would I celebrate with?"

"I don't know, a pretty girl comes to mind right off the bat."

Darrel shrugged. "I'll keep that in mind for next time. Did you have any girls in particular in mind?"

"Let's talk about that outside, too," Jimmy said. "At least let me tip the dogs."

That was how my regulars referred to my jar. "Okay, but don't go too crazy."

After Jimmy shoved a five in the jar, I watched as the two men walked to the front register together, all the while talking about something. I wanted to abandon my station and follow them, but if I even thought about doing that, I'd have a riot on my hands.

It was something to keep in mind, though.

I cleared away their dirty dishes into a bin I kept behind the bar, wiped down the counter where the two men had just been sitting, and then I invited the next two diners to join me. There really wasn't a formal line as such, but I knew for a fact that my patrons were well aware of who was next, and heaven help the diner who tried to skip ahead out of sequence.

"Ten more minutes on the breakfast menu, folks," I told them as I pointed to the board mounted to the wall. I'd tried one on an easel at first, but it had taken up too much valuable space, so I'd switched to the current method. I'd had to learn to write legibly while leaning over the counter, but it was a much better system.

"I don't suppose lunch is ready yet, is it?" Margaret Wilson asked me as she frowned at the menu. She had taught me in the third grade, and something that I'd always cherished about her was that she'd never talked down to me, even way back then.

"I'm sorry, ma'am. It's not due to be served for another ten minutes," I said loudly, and then I winked at her. With a whisper, I added, "If you and Larry would like some chamomile tea while you're deciding, you should be just fine, though." Her husband had been a teacher at my elementary school as well, though I'd never had any classes with him. Maybe that was why

I could call him by his first name now, while his spouse would always be Mrs. Wilson to me.

"That sounds lovely," my former teacher said. "What are we having today?"

"I've got some wonderful chickens in the oven roasting with carrots, potatoes, and onions in two of my Dutch ovens, and some ribs, onions, and bell peppers in another. There will be cornbread, too, and if it turns out okay, I'll have some pineapple upside down cake available as well."

She smiled broadly at the news and then turned to her husband. "Shall we order one of each and share?"

"Sounds good to me," he said with a smile.

"Excellent," Mrs. Wilson said. I always had a pot of hot water simmering away on the back burner of my range, so preparing the tea was simplicity itself. After I poured two cups for them, I served them with lemon wedges and milk, something I knew that Mrs. Wilson preferred.

"Thank you, my dear," she told me before taking a sip of her tea. "It's wonderful."

"Glad you like it," I said as I turned back to my grill. "I'll serve you shortly."

"No hurries, no worries," Larry said. His disposition matched his wife's beautifully, and I doubted that the two of them had ever raised their voices in each other's company. I knew that some of my friends thought that arguments were required to have a good relationship, but I didn't think so. My folks had shared the same kind of relationship as the couple in front of me, and if their lives hadn't been ended so abruptly by a hit-and-run driver, I knew in my heart that they would still be together. The only negative I could see from being such a close observer of that tranquil a relationship was that it set the bar rather high for me and my siblings. Was that why Kathleen, Pat, and I had yet to find significant others in our lives? I hoped not. Someday, I wanted what my parents and the Wilsons shared.

"How are you dealing with the morning's events?" Mrs. Wilson asked me as I served Les Hodges his eggs and sausage nearby.

"I'm okay," I said.

"It must have been quite a shock," Larry chimed in. "Has Franklin been by?"

"No, not that I'm aware of," I said. Franklin Davis was Chester's older brother. He could put on a nice front when it suited his needs, but I'd never been a fan of the man.

"That surprises me," Larry said with a frown.

"Why is that?"

"You might not realize it, but Franklin was protective of his little brother back in school, at least where other people were concerned. While he considered it his right to beat on Chester whenever it pleased him, no one dared touch his little brother, or they would have to face Franklin's wrath."

"That's an odd way to act," I said.

"That was Franklin to a tee. That's why I figured that he'd be over here demanding somebody's head by now."

"Is there a possibility that no one's told him yet?" Mrs. Wilson asked. "That's a ghastly thought to consider."

"I'm certain that Kathleen has spoken to him by now," I replied.

"I hope so. It would be a dreadful thing to discover by accident."

I agreed with my former teacher, and I wondered if I should call Kathleen and ask her if she'd spoken to Franklin yet. No, she'd think I was meddling, and since it was true that I was actually digging into the murder behind her back, she would have been right. I decided to let that particular detail go and hope that she'd chatted with him by now anyway.

"As for me, I'm curious if anyone's told Harper Gentry yet," Les said, clearly eavesdropping on our conversation. In his defense, everyone was jammed fairly tightly into a relatively small space, so it was difficult not to overhear half a dozen conversations.

"Why should anyone tell Harper anything?" Larry asked him.

"Hadn't you heard? They must have been dating. At least that's what I figured after what I saw."

"What did you see?" I asked, unable to help myself.

"All I know is that the two of them were in the park last night arguing like a couple of teenagers," he said.

"They were fighting? Then what makes you think that they were dating?" Mrs. Wilson asked.

"Trust me, nobody has that much passion in a fight unless there's love behind it," he said knowingly.

"It sounds like you're speaking from experience," Sally Tremont observed from Les's other side.

"You know it," Les said with a grin.

"Lester Dale Hodges, you don't know what you're talking about, as usual," Sally said matter-of-factly, and then she pressed her lips tightly together.

"Sally, when are you going to let it go? We went out once, it didn't work out, so we went our separate ways," Les said with a wicked grin. "Can I help it if I didn't fall in love with you like you did with me?"

Sally's face turned such a bright shade of red that for a moment, I thought she might be having a heart attack. "Lester, you take that back!"

It was loud enough to stop every other conversation in the Iron, even the ones that hadn't been close enough to hear what had been going on.

"I'm sorry," Les mumbled. He'd crossed a line, and he knew it.

"I didn't hear you. You'll have to repeat that," Sally said forcefully.

Was she really going to make him say it again?

"I said that I was sorry," Les said a little louder that time. He was suitably chastised, but Sally wasn't showing any signs of letting up. I had to stop this before it got even uglier. I plucked up Sally's check and handed it to Les. "Sally, Les will be happy to buy you breakfast if you promise to drop it right now. Won't you, Les?" I asked as I stared hard at him.

"Of course I will. I said that I was sorry."

"Sally? Do you accept his apology?" I asked her just as firmly.

I knew that she wanted to continue punishing him, but it was just as obvious that Sally realized that I wasn't messing around, either. After all, I had the power to ban her from ever eating at my grill again, and I knew for a fact that the woman couldn't boil water with an instruction manual to help her. If I cut her off, she'd starve in a matter of days.

"That would be acceptable," she said primly, and then, with a wicked grin, she asked me, "Can I order a few things to go?"

"You may not," I said, but I winked at her to soften the sting of my refusal.

To my surprise, Sally winked back. "Hey, you can't blame me for trying." She stood, and then, on what was clearly pure impulse, she leaned down and kissed Les soundly on the lips. After taking a moment to catch her breath, I heard her say to him softly, "If I'd wanted you, I could have had you at the drop of a hat."

She left to a round of applause, and after a moment, Les joined in as well with a grin of his own. He stood to leave as well, and for the first time I could remember, there was food left on his plate.

"You don't need to rush off," I told him as he took both checks.

"I can't stay. There's something I need to do," Les said. I watched as he practically threw his money at Pat, and then he hurried out the door, no doubt in search of Sally to continue their conversation.

I chuckled as I cleaned their spots away, wiped the counter again, and made room for two more diners.

I'd learned a great deal from many of the earlier exchanges, and I couldn't help but wonder what clues might come my way the rest of the day.

CHAPTER 8: PAT

A NNIE WAS A JOY TO watch as she worked at her grill. It was almost like watching a well-choreographed dance, the way she went from station to station in constant fluid motion. My twin sister had a real knack for taking the simplest ingredients and turning them into culinary masterpieces. Not that everything she made was perfect, especially when she was trying out new recipes. When that was going on, she needed every bit of power the massive range hood over her cooking station had in it to clear away the smoke at times. The truth was that I usually didn't mind being her guinea pig. After all, it meant that I was often the first person to taste her new creations. Plus, I got to offer suggestions, and finally, when she made something for me to eat, I didn't have to cook for myself, so I could head straight up to my apartment upstairs after everyone else left for the day. I knew Annie thought I was crazy to want to live above the Iron, but it was perfect for me, just as her cabin in the woods suited her ideally.

I headed for the back door, vowing to be as quick as I could manage. It was time to see how Kathleen was progressing with her investigation, and after stationing Skip up front at the register, I felt fairly confident deserting my post, at least for the two minutes my task should take.

Boy, did I underestimate that particular time line.

"Stop right where you are! I want to talk to you!" I shouted as I rushed after the figure fleeing into the dense woods beside the shop. Though it was broad daylight, the tree canopy cut off a great deal of sunlight, and I couldn't get much detail about who had been lurking there. I wasn't even sure if it was a man or a woman. In all honesty, it might have been perfectly harmless, but if that was the case, why did the person run the moment I stepped outside? What had they been doing skulking about and, more importantly, had they achieved their objective, or had I scared them off before they could manage it?

Kathleen came around the side of the building just as I started after the trespasser.

"What are you yelling about, Pat? I heard you all the way up front."

"Someone was watching the Iron from the woods, and when I spotted them, they took off running." I tried to keep going after whoever it was, but Kathleen put a restraining hand on my shoulder.

"Forget it. Whoever was there is long gone by now."

I looked into the trees and saw that she was right. "Why would someone sneak around the Iron like that?"

"Are you positive they were watching this place?" she asked me.

"What else could they have been doing, and more importantly, why did they run away when I caught them spying on us?"

"Pat, it was probably just someone too embarrassed about being caught creeping around a crime scene. You'd be amazed how many looky-loos we get. I'm sure that it was nothing."

"Maybe you're right," I conceded, though I still had my doubts. It had something to do with the murder; I just knew it, even though I didn't have any empirical evidence to substantiate it. I wanted to snoop around among the trees just in case our visitor had dropped something, but I couldn't do it with my sister, the sheriff, standing right there. "Have you wrapped things up yet out front?"

"We have," she admitted. "That was why I was headed inside. You can have the front porch of the Iron back."

I glanced at my watch. "Wow, that was an hour faster than I was expecting."

"I could always keep someone out there for another sixty minutes," she said with a slight grin. "Funny, I thought you'd be pleased."

"I am," I said quickly. "I guess this thing's just got me spooked."

"I'd say that's a pretty typical reaction to murder. How's Annie holding up?"

"You could always go inside and ask her yourself," I said.

"I could, but I'm not sure she would tell me anything. The two of you have had something between you since you were born. It's an odd thing to feel like an outsider in your own family." She said it almost wistfully, as though it was a sad truth that she'd come to accept a long time ago.

"Kathleen, you know that we never meant to exclude you," I said gently. My older sister could be rough around the edges at times, and she could be too quick to judge on occasion, but she had a good heart, and I loved her. The very idea that Annie and I had made her feel unwelcome in her own family was appalling to me.

"I know you didn't, and I love you both despite everything," she answered with a smile as she patted my cheek. "How could you help it? You two have every right to be as close as two siblings can be. I never resented either one of you for it, but I wished that I'd been a twin myself more than once when we were growing up."

"I'm not sure the world could handle two of you," I said with a smile.

"Now that I think about it, neither am I," she said, joining me with a broader grin of her own. "Keep an eye on Annie, okay? I'm afraid she's going to get some kind of delayed shock when she realizes what she saw this morning."

"I'll do what I can, but I'm not sleeping out in that cabin with her, no matter what," I replied. "There's only so much I'm willing to do for either one of my sisters."

"You're a real city slicker at heart, aren't you?"

I shrugged. "What can I say? I like to be surrounded by civilization, and I enjoy the creature comforts of my home."

"You mean your attic?" she asked as she laughed. "Is it really that much different from Annie's cabin?"

"I think so. For one thing, there's not much danger of a bear coming to my front door when I live here over the Iron," I said.

"To be fair, Annie's never seen one out there, either."

"Not yet, anyway. It's still early, so give it time. We were going to go our separate ways this evening, but should we change our plans? The three of us could have dinner together, if you'd like."

"Don't you have to check with Annie first before you make an offer like that? What if she's got a date?"

"The last time she went out was New Year's Eve last year, and that was such a disaster, she swears she's giving up on finding anyone."

"Just wait. She'll meet someone, and so will you."

"I'm about ready to throw in the towel myself. After Molly broke my heart, I haven't much felt like going out. First dates are too much like job interviews, you know what I mean? Besides, what about you? Boy, the Marshes aren't exactly burning up the dating world these days, are we?"

"I don't have time to date," she said tersely. "I'm married to my job."

"Surely there's someone you'd like to go out with."

"I lock up most of the men I meet," Kathleen said with

a shrug. "Thanks for the offer, but I'll have to pass on your gracious dinner invitation. I've got a murder to solve."

"Sorry we can't help you with that," I said lightly, trying to keep my guilt about working on the case behind her back to myself.

"You stick to what you know, and I'll do the same."

As Kathleen headed back up front, I followed her a minute later to confirm that she and her deputies were actually leaving. When I saw the squad cars pull away, I headed straight for the woods beside us instead of going back into the Iron. I just hoped that Skip wasn't giving away the entire store, literally.

I was about to give up my search of the copse of trees and go back inside when I noticed that something was stuck to one of my shoes. Annie and I both wore running shoes at work, since we were on our feet all day. Besides, we didn't have a dress code, or a boss to answer to, so we could pretty much wear what we wanted. I leaned against a tree and held up my shoe. It was a piece of paper, torn so that I only had part of it, but the fragment I found was enough to get my heart racing.

In block letters printed in heavy pencil, it said,

COME TO THE IRON BY SIX TOMORROW MORNING, OR I'LL—

I had no idea what the note's author would do, but I had a hunch that it had something to do with Chester's murder.

I had to show this to Annie and see what she thought about it. I knew enough not to handle the paper too much. If there were fingerprints on it, I didn't want to smudge them and possibly ruin a clue. I tucked it carefully in my handkerchief, a blue paisley bandana, and I headed back inside.

I wanted to show the note to my sister as soon as I got back inside the Iron, but she was busy cooking late meals for a dozen customers, and besides, it appeared as though Skip was having problems up front.

I made my way to the front of the store and found Virgil Hicks, as ornery and contrary a man as you'd ever want to meet. "What's going on?" I asked as I joined Skip behind the long counter.

"He shorted me ten dollars!" Virgil snapped, "That's what's going on. I want my money, and I want it right this second, or I'll call that big sister of yours and have this snotty kid arrested for theft."

"He gave me a ten for a nine dollar and eighty-seven cent purchase," Skip said, a hint of a quiver in his voice. "I wouldn't cheat him."

"If you're already a thief, why should I believe that you wouldn't be a liar, too?"

"Virgil, keep your voice down," I said in the calmest demeanor I could muster.

"You can't shut me up, Patrick Marsh!"

I leaned over the counter. "Last warning. Either be civil or find someplace else to eat your meals, buy your groceries and hardware, and get your mail delivered."

Virgil didn't like the implication that I might ban him, so at least he lowered his voice. "You can't bully me. I won't stand for it."

"I'm not bullying you," I said. A few folks were watching us closely, waiting to see what would happen next. I had no interest in putting on a show. I reached for my wallet and pulled out a ten-dollar bill.

As I handed it to Virgil, Skip said, "I didn't cheat him, Pat! That's the truth!"

"It's okay, young fellow," Virgil said, clearly feeling pleased with himself. "Everybody makes mistakes. You're only human."

"So are you, Virgil," I said. There were two folks waiting to pay for their meals and shopping items. "Sorry for the inconvenience, but unless you've got exact change or you're using a credit card, there's going to be a slight delay."

"Why can't we pay now, Pat?" Madeline Vance asked.

"I have to run a report on the register and balance out my till," I said. "It's the only way I'm going to know who's right. It won't take long, I promise."

"Do what you must," she said. "I wouldn't say no to having a little more time to shop."

I started to pull out the till when I looked hard at Virgil one last time. "Fair warning. If the register balances out, you and I are going to have a problem, and I'll be needing that ten back. Are you absolutely certain that you gave Skip a twenty and not a ten?"

His face clouded up for a moment before he spoke. "I'm pretty sure," he finally said grudgingly.

"Well, I'm one hundred percent sure that it was a ten," Skip said defiantly.

"Not now," I said to him in a hard voice. There was a time to stand up for himself, but this wasn't it, not while I was making a point. I believed my employee. This wasn't the first time Virgil had tried to pull something tricky over on us, but it was going to be the last if I had anything to say about it. If the register did indeed turn up to be balanced after I'd given him ten dollars out of my own wallet, Virgil was going to see what things were like looking in from the outside. I knew that I couldn't ban him forever, but two or three days away from the Iron might be enough to teach him a lesson about trying to take advantage of me or my staff. "Virgil, it's your call."

He frowned again, then he reached for his wallet and pulled out the ten I'd just given him. "Go on. Take it."

I left it on the counter where he'd just slammed it down. "No, thanks." I finished pulling the till out so I could count the money, and then I reached for my cash register keys. I loved this register; I could run all kinds of reports on it, many of which I never used, but come the end of the day, I always matched my day's take with what the register reported, and I was never off by more than a few pennies one way or the other.

"I said take it," Virgil insisted as he pushed it toward me.

"If it's not given willingly, and you're not going to admit that you made an honest mistake, I don't have any choice."

"I made a mistake," Virgil said in a near whisper. "Is that good enough for you?"

It wasn't, not by a long shot. "Apologize."

"Pat, I'm sorry for the confusion. Sometimes I—"

"To him, not to me," I said as I interrupted him and pointed to my employee.

"You're kidding," Virgil said distastefully.

"It's okay, Pat," Skip cut in. "I don't need it."

"Well, I think you do," I said. "Virgil?"

"I'm sorry." He spoke the words as though each one cost him money.

I looked at Skip. "Is that okay?"

"Fine," he said.

"Good," I replied as I put the till back in place. I hoped and prayed that when I cashed out the register at the end of the day, we weren't ten dollars over what we should have had. If we were, Skip was going to have to make a pretty painful apology himself, but in the meantime, it was time to get business back to normal. Pretending nothing had happened, I smiled at Virgil and asked, "Can you believe the state legislature voted to increase the gas tax again yesterday?"

It was an olive branch, and he knew it. I wasn't sure that he was going to take it for a second, but then Virgil rose to the occasion. "Pat, I've told you for years, they're all a bunch of crooks, with one hand out and the other reaching for our wallets. There ought to be a law against them."

"Maybe you could run for office and show them how it should be done, Virgil," Skip said with a smile, getting into the spirit of reconciliation.

That made Virgil grin. "Skip, they wouldn't know what to do with me, I can guarantee you that, but I like the way you think, young man."

After Virgil was gone, Skip looked at me intently once we were alone again. "Thanks for backing me up, Pat."

"It was the right thing to do. He had no right to come after you like that, and it's not like it's the first time Virgil's tried something. I think he does it just to show the world that he's still got a bite to go along with his bark."

"If anyone's not sure about that, they can just ask me," Skip said as he glanced at the clock. "Just ten minutes until we close."

"You can take off early if you want to," I said as I busied myself straightening up the checkout counter. "It's okay by me."

"Thanks, but if it's all the same to you, I'll stick around until the end of the day."

I noticed a worried look in his eyes. "You want to see how the report balances, don't you?"

"I'm sure that I'm right," he insisted, "but I'd still like to get confirmation of it, if you know what I mean."

"I understand. Why don't you stock the bread and the one-inch U-bolts? Both of them are getting low."

"I can do that," he said happily.

As soon as I had Skip out from under my feet, I raised all

the shades we'd lowered earlier, walked around the counter, and opened the front door. It would be nice having our main access back, if only for a few moments. As I unlocked the door, I was surprised to find a man around my age in a three-piece suit standing there. I didn't recognize him, and that was saying something in our little town. It wasn't exactly tourist season, and even if it were, he wasn't dressed like most of the folks we got who explored the mountains around us in the summer. "Welcome to the Iron! Come on in," I said as I held the door open for him. "If we don't have it, the truth is that you probably don't need it."

"Are you Mr. Patrick Marsh?" he asked with a slight frown.

"Guilty as charged," I said as I offered my hand.

"And your sister, Analeigh Marsh? Is she present as well?"

"She is," I said as I pointed back to her grill, where she was working. "I've got the feeling you're not here to shop. What is this about?"

"My name is G. Robert Benton III, and I need fifteen uninterrupted minutes of your time," he said as he handed me a heavily embossed business card that described him as an attorney at law.

"I'd like a pony, myself," I said, "but I don't think either one of us is going to get what we're wishing for, at least not at this very second."

He looked confused by my reply. "I assure you, it's important."

"Mr. Benton, we close in eight minutes," I said. "After that, Annie and I need another fifteen to button things up for the day. If you'd like to come back in half an hour, we might be able to help you, but until then, we won't be able to cooperate."

"Don't you want to know what brings me here?" he asked.

"I figure you'll get around to it sooner or later, but at the moment, unless you have a warrant for our arrests, we're willing to wait to find out."

He looked truly puzzled by my response. "I'll be back in thirty minutes."

"See you then," I said as I turned back inside. He was right about one thing: I was dying to know why he was at the Iron looking for my twin and me, but I wasn't going to give him the satisfaction of hearing me ask. I hadn't been joking; Annie and I had a great deal to do, and we didn't need any interruptions unless the situation was clearly more dire than it was being presented by the attorney.

I waited to tell my twin sister what had happened until we'd shooed our last customer out through the front door. Edith had left her station at two as was her regular routine, but Skip was still there, looking at the register anxiously every chance he got. After the front door was dead bolted and the signs were all flipped over to show the world that we were finished for the day, I started counting the money in the till as the register ran its report. I had my tally before the machine quit chugging out its numbers, and Skip began to edge closer and closer, as though it were a predator he was too afraid to approach.

"How's it look, Pat?" he finally asked.

"Too soon to tell just yet," I replied, trying to keep my voice calm and level. I surely hoped that he'd been right. The last thing I wanted to deal with was Virgil's righteous indignation if I had to tell him that we'd made a mistake after all.

The register finally stopped, and I scanned the tape for the day's cash balance line, the only one that I cared about at the moment.

It matched the physical tally to the dime.

I grinned at Skip and gave him two thumbs up.

"Wow, that's a relief," he said, and then he quickly amended, "Not that I wasn't sure before."

"I agree, it's good having official confirmation," I said with a smile. "Now get out of here."

"Yes, sir. Happy to."

After I made out our daily deposit slip and put the cash and receipts in the zippered bag we used, I glanced at my watch and saw that we had seven minutes before the attorney was due back.

It was time to catch my sister up on what had happened, what I'd found outside, and what was to come.

CHAPTER 9: ANNIE

"**S**O THAT'S WHERE THINGS STAND right now," Pat said as he finished telling me about what had happened from his end of things during the afternoon.

"Let me see that note again," I said as I reached out my hand.

"Be careful, Annie. We shouldn't get any fingerprints on it," Pat replied.

"I'm pretty sure that you aren't doing it any good wrapping it up in your bandana like that," I countered. "Hang on a second. I've got an idea." I went behind my counter and pulled out a baggie I used for leftovers sometimes. "Put it in here if you want to take good care of it."

"That's a good idea. Why didn't I think of that?"

"That's why there are two of us," I answered. He gently worked the note from his bandana into the baggie, and I sealed it shut. After that, I studied it a little more closely than I'd been able to before. "This isn't just plain paper."

"I noticed that, too. Do you have any idea where it might have come from? Because I'm stumped."

"I'm not sure, either," I said. "And you're sure you didn't get a good look at our lurker?"

"Annie, I'm not any happier about it than you are. I might have missed the pivotal clue that would have solved this case."

"Don't be so hard on yourself, Pat," I said as I gently touched my brother's shoulder. "I know how dense those woods can be.

I keep telling you that we should buy the lot and turn it into an overflow parking lot."

He laughed at me. "That sounds kind of ironic coming from a nature-lover like you."

"I didn't say that we should clear-cut it. I'd just like to have enough space for *all* of our customers to be able to park when they want to pay us a visit. We could make it into a park if we did it right."

"Where are we going to get the money to buy it?" he asked me. "How many offers have we already made to Molly?"

"I'm pretty sure you could persuade her to sell if you put your mind to it." My brother was hopelessly in love with his ex-girlfriend, and everyone in town knew it, with one notable exception. Molly acted as though she had no idea, and I had a feeling that she reciprocated his emotions, but Pat had warned me sternly not to meddle, and he'd used a tone of voice that I knew better than to defy. They'd just have to muddle their own way out of it, or not. I was mum on the subject.

"It's not going to happen, no matter how much all of Maple Crest might want it to," Pat replied. "We'll be fine the way things stand."

"If you say so," I said. "Did you have any idea that so many people would want to see Chester come to harm? Because I know that I didn't."

"I'd hate for someone to make a list of the folks who'd want to see something bad happen to me," Pat said a little tentatively. "Wouldn't you?"

I laughed before I answered his question. "Why would anyone in the world want to harm me? I spread sunshine wherever I go."

He chuckled with me, which had been my goal. Sure, I'd been the one to find Chester's body and had it pin me to the ground, but it was important that I didn't forget that Pat had been the one who'd rolled his body off me. It had to have hit him hard, too, and it was worrying me a little that he hadn't shown more emotion than he had after it had happened. Would he break down in the middle of the night when he was all alone? I couldn't imagine that situation being any healthier for him than to have it happen when I was around so that I could at least offer him a little comfort. Kathleen knew how close my twin and I were, and I knew that she'd help with Pat if she could, but I wasn't even sure that my presence would alleviate the situation. My brother and I were what we were, two people who had originated at the exact same moment in time in the exact same place, but in some ways, we were anything but twins.

"Sis, you really don't believe that bit about you being all goodness and light, do you?" Pat asked me, though his grin was still present.

"The way I look at it is that if it helps me sleep at night, why shouldn't I?" I asked him. "I wonder what this lawyer wants from the two of us. Nobody's suing us, are they?"

"It wouldn't surprise me one bit if they were, given the world we live in," Pat said. "But I don't think that's it."

"Why not?"

"It's hard to explain. I guess it was because he didn't have that look about him," Pat answered. "He was here on a more puzzling mission, if you ask me. I wasn't entirely sure that he knew what he was doing here any more than I did."

"I suppose we'll find out soon enough. As a matter of fact, I think I just heard a car pull into the lot, and our regular customers know that when we're closed, that's exactly what we mean."

Thirty seconds later, there was a series of raps on the front door, and Pat and I went to open it together. When I saw the man standing there, I realized that my brother hadn't told me that the attorney was kind of cute.

"Well, if it isn't my old friend, G. Robert Benton III," Pat said as he held the door open for him.

He looked at my brother skeptically, and then he offered me a slight smile as well as his hand. "You must be Analeigh."

"Annie is fine," I said as I smiled at him. The hand I shook was firm, and the other wasn't wearing a wedding ring. Two pluses for the attorney.

"You can just call me Rob," he said, and then he caught himself and put on a more formal air. "Do you both have time for me now?"

"We have all that you need," I said as I ushered him inside.

Pat raised an eyebrow in my direction, and I gave him a look that said he'd better not get cute. Right now, that was my job.

"What exactly can we do for you, Rob?" Pat asked, and I could see the attorney flinch a little at hearing his first name spoken by my brother. No doubt he'd meant that I could call him by name, but not my brother. Still, he was stuck with it, and I could see from his expression that he was going to accept it as graciously as he could manage.

"I understand you two found Mr. Davis's body this morning. Is that correct?"

"It is," I said.

"I'm sorry that you had to go through that," Rob said sympathetically. "Mr. Davis was a friend of mine, and he spoke highly of the two of you."

"What a nice thing to say," I replied. "Though I can't imagine why our names would come up in conversation with you. Chester was our customer and our friend, but in the end, we weren't really all that close."

"He begged to differ," the attorney said. "In fact, I got instructions from him just last night that in case something were to happen to him, I should speak with you both immediately."

"Was there anything in particular he wanted you to tell us?" I asked him.

"I'm not privy to that information, I'm afraid."

"Then why exactly are you here?" Pat asked him bluntly as he headed for the front door. "We appreciate you extending your sympathies to us and all that, but it's been a long day, so if you'll excuse us..."

It was clearly an attempt to get rid of the attorney, but Rob was having none of it. Instead of walking toward the door with Pat, which was clearly my brother's intention, the attorney used the counter up front to rest his briefcase on. When he unlatched it with two sharp clicks, I felt a jolt run through me. It was as though something ominous had just been unleashed into the air, no matter how ridiculous that would have sounded if I'd dared to say it aloud. I'm not saying there were puffs of smoke, or hissing, or even a cloud of despair. I'm just saying that I had the feeling that I wasn't going to like whatever was about to come out.

"Chester Davis was under the strong impression last night that someone was going to try to kill him," the attorney said matter-of-factly. If he'd embellished the news, or played it for what it was worth, I might have dismissed it, but his statement was so mundane that I had no choice but to take it seriously.

"What exactly did he say?" Pat asked the attorney.

"I'm sorry, but that's privileged, even with my client's demise."

"Then I'll ask you again. If you can't talk to us, then why are you here?"

"Before Mr. Davis called me, he informed me that he'd written two letters. Actually, he just wrote one, but he instructed me to make a copy of it without reading it and to deliver both copies to the two of you if anything happened to him. He said that you weren't always willing to share and that it would make matters easier if I presented you each with a letter of your own."

As he handed us our envelopes, I asked, "And you weren't even tempted to peek while you were making a copy?"

He smiled, and I could see dimples suddenly appear. *Focus,*

Annie. You can daydream about this man later when you have more time and opportunity.

"I'm willing to admit that I was tempted, but I respected Mr. Davis's wishes."

After we each had our letter, Pat asked without opening his, "Was there anything else?"

It was clear that the attorney had hoped to learn of the letters' contents when we opened our envelopes, but it became just as clear that wasn't going to happen. I was with Pat on that one hundred percent. Rob might be handsome, but this was something else entirely—what, I didn't know just yet.

"No, that will be all for now, but we'll need to speak again soon." He handed me his business card, since he'd already given Pat one, the same one my brother had shown me when he'd told me about the attorney's earlier visit. "If you need me in the interim, and I mean for anything, please don't hesitate to call."

"I'm sorry we had to meet in these trying circumstances," I said as my brother and I walked him to the door and showed him out.

The man just shrugged. He was about to say something else when my brother closed the door firmly in his face.

"Was that entirely necessary?" I asked him.

"I did you a favor. I didn't want you to embarrass yourself," Pat said.

"I'm sure that I don't know what you're talking about," I answered stiffly.

"Sure, okay, whatever you say," Pat replied. "I wonder what Chester had to tell us that was so important that he had to communicate with us from beyond the grave."

"I guess that there's only one way to find out," I said as I ripped my envelope open, unfolded the letter, and began to read.

CHAPTER 10: CHESTER'S LETTER

T WINS, IF YOU'RE READING MY *letter, then it turns out that I was right. You should know that I take little consolation in that. Thirty-nine is too young to tell the world good-bye, but then again, if I were in my eighties, I'd probably feel the exact same way. I can tell you both that it's a fact that being right isn't all it's cracked up to be. I bet you are both dying to know what this is about. The truth of the matter is that I'm not absolutely certain about that myself. Either somebody's tried to kill me twice already, and is going for "third time's the charm" tomorrow morning, or I have an extremely overactive imagination. I'm going to have to ask you two to be the judges of that for yourselves. Why you two, you might ask? It came to me an hour ago. There aren't a great many people in this world that I trust, but you are two of them. While you both have your own idiosyncrasies—and let's be honest, who doesn't—I know that I can count on you to dig into this and find out who killed me tomorrow morning, and why. I'm sure I just gave an English major a stroke with that sentence, but who cares? This is real life, and I'm long past caring. That's the thing, though. I'm not. I know, or at least I greatly suspect, that I won't learn the outcome of what you are both about to do for me, but it matters to me here and now. That's all that I can say.*

Find out who killed me, and just as important, why they did it.

Why would you agree to do this last favor for me while your sister is the sheriff in these parts? I have a high opinion of Kathleen, and as a basic law enforcement officer, she's the tops. But whoever did this is going to be clever, and I have a hunch that if normal channels are all that are used to catch my soon-to-be killer, someone's going to quite literally get away with murder.

Oh, I almost forgot. After I sign off, I'll list the folks I suspect and why, so you won't be starting from scratch. Then I'll give you more details about the attempts on my life so far.

One last thing about Rob. I'll be honest with you; I don't know what to think about the man anymore. Good guy or bad, I can't say, whether it has something to do with him, or if it's just this paranoid man letting his imagination run wild.

In the meantime, happy hunting.

And be careful.

Remember, whoever killed me is smarter than the average bear, and I'd hate to think that I was throwing you into the path of an oncoming freight train. I just mixed metaphors there, didn't I? Who knows, maybe the bear's driving the train, or maybe my words are just the ramblings of a man facing his own mortality.

If this is a false alarm, I'll tear this letter up tomorrow at lunch and have a good laugh at myself.

If it's not, then you two know what to do.

I'm counting on you both, Annie and Pat.

Don't let me down.

All my very best to you both,

I'm proud to say, your friend,

Chester

As promised, there was another page included in the letter.

Chester had certainly been thorough. It must have broken his heart to sum up his life by listing the people closest to him who might want to see him dead.

Let's see. If I'm listing people who might want to see me dead, there's no better place to start than my very own brother. Franklin has had a mean streak in him since the day he came out of the womb, and most of his anger in life has seemed to be directed toward me. At least he spared Lydia most of that particular pain. My baby sister and I had very different childhoods, though we grew up in the same home just eleven months apart. Franklin has been jealous of my success his entire life, from our time in school all the way to today. I made better grades, better money, better investments, and was better at just about everything, and I suspect that he never forgave me for surpassing him in every way. He's so arrogant that he probably still believes that he's in my will, though I've told him a hundred times that I've scratched his name out. I lied, though. He's going to get a piece of everything that I own, twenty-five percent, to be exact. I know he's going to fuss and fume about even that. There's no doubt in my mind that he expects it all. You may wonder why I should give him anything. I bought my first land with a loan from our mother and father. They didn't want me to pay the money back. All they'd asked in return was that someday I would promise to look out for my older brother and younger sister. I wish they'd taken the money, but they wouldn't hear of it, so this is my way of fulfilling my last obligation, something I admittedly had a tough time doing while I was alive.

Should Lydia be on the list, too? I wish I could say for sure one way or the other, but I can't. She was a complicated little girl, and that didn't change when she grew up. I don't know if you realize this or not, but my little sister married for money all three times, and never for love, at least as far as I could tell. She is driven by greed more than any one person I could name, and if she believed that she was going to inherit much more than a postage stamp from me, she might have done it, as much as it pains me to admit it. I doubt that she'll be all that happy with just twenty-five percent, either, but it is what it is.

I'm guessing that you're going to think that Julia, my ex-wife, should be next, but I'm not so sure about her. I know for a fact that she loved me, once upon a time; of that there is no doubt. I guess a part of me has always loved her, too. She's in my will, and she knows it. Is ten percent of what I have enough to kill for? I don't know. Could she have done it? It's probably worth looking into.

Bryson Oak, on the other hand, has deservedly earned himself a spot near the top of your list. The two of us have had an unhealthy relationship since we were in school, and I'm ashamed to admit that if there was ever a chance to screw him over, I always took it gladly. If anyone had a reason to want to see the end of me, Bryson would certainly qualify.

The last name on my list has to be Harper Gentry's. I've been going out with Harper for awhile now. What can I say? We have a complicated relationship; things constantly seem to run hot or cold between us. When we're getting along, it's amazing, but when we're not, it makes me rethink the entire arrangement. In case you're wondering, she's getting ten percent herself, so that most likely gives her a motive, too.

And that's it for my list of suspects.

It amazes me even now just how shameful this process of self-examination has been for me, and if I live through the next attempt on my life, I'm vowing right here and now to try to do better by the folks around me and to make amends wherever it's possible. I believe that I'll be judged for my actions sooner rather than later, and I'll accept my fate, whatever it might be, but I truly wish there was more time to make things right with the people in my life.

And now here are the details about what has happened so far. As far as I can tell, there have been two separate attempts on my life in the past week. Six days ago, I was out for my standard early-morning walk to the Iron when a car approached from behind me. It was still dark out, but they didn't have their lights on. Almost too late, I noticed the car barreling toward me, and at the last moment, I jumped off the road and into the trees. If I hadn't been paying attention, there's no doubt in my mind that I'd be dead now. Hang on, that doesn't make sense, because if you're reading this, I'm dead, anyway. You understand what I mean. The car was one of those big dark ominous machines, like it was capable of transporting storm troopers or something. Have you ever been behind an Escalade or a Denali and tried to see around them? It's a nightmare. If that thing had hit me, there wouldn't have been enough left to bury.

The second attempt was when I was checking out one of my properties outside of town. I'll bet you didn't know that I owned 828 acres all around Maple Crest. I've acquired it slowly and steadily, and as far as I know, I'm the biggest land baron in town, if you can believe that. That acreage was picked up mostly on the cheap, but a great deal of it's worth a fortune now. Anyway, I was out walking the land because someone had tipped me off anonymously that a thief was clear-cutting my acreage. I was deep in the heart of the woods without seeing any signs that it was true when I heard a shot being fired. An instant later, a chunk of bark flew off the tree trunk beside me. I ducked down for cover just as the second shot hit over my head. Somebody was clearly after me, but what they didn't realize was that I was armed myself, just in case there was a confrontation with this supposed thief. I fired a shot in the general direction of where the two shots had come from, and I was about to investigate when I heard a car in the distance driving off like a madman. I know in my heart that there was nothing accidental about the shooting. So why didn't I tell anyone, not even your sister? Stubborn pride, I guess, or maybe I just realized how futile it would be to bring the police into it after the fact. After that, I started watching my back wherever I went, but evidently, I wasn't quite vigilant enough if you both are reading these letters right now.

Like I said before, the killer's crafty, so be careful.

And that about sums everything up.

All I ask is that you both do the best that you can. Know that I'll appreciate it more than I could ever tell you, and don't worry. If you should decide not to help me out after reading all of this, well, I don't suppose that I can blame you a bit. It was worth a shot asking you, though.

No matter what, please remember that you had my true friendship in life, and my gratitude for all of the little kindnesses you did for me over the course of our association.

Your friend for all of eternity,

Chester

CHAPTER 11: PAT

"**W**HAT DO YOU THINK ABOUT all of this, Annie?" I asked my sister as I finished my copy of the letter. She'd always been a faster reader than me, so I wasn't surprised to see that she was already done with hers.

"To be honest with you, I'm more determined than ever to find Chester's killer," she said.

I tapped the letter in my hand on the counter. "Shouldn't we share this with Kathleen?"

"No. Absolutely not."

I looked at her to see if she was smiling, but there was no expression on her face. "You're kidding, right?"

"Pat, think about it. If Chester had wanted her to know what we know, he would have sent her a letter, too. If she did get one, Chester didn't mention it, and neither did Rob."

"Speaking of the attorney, were you seriously hitting on him when he was here?"

"I was just being polite," Annie said.

"And there was nothing more to it than that?"

She didn't even dignify my question with a response, but that didn't necessarily mean that I was wrong. Annie hadn't been the luckiest when it came to love, but then again, neither had I. While I'd spent the last few years falling in and out of love with Molly, Annie had dated a few men casually, not a single one of them good enough for her, at least in my opinion. Maybe I should have backed off saying anything about the attorney. If she wanted to see him, it was none of my business. Being a twin entitled me to only so much information about her life, because it was reciprocal as well. If I kept badgering her about her love interests, it wouldn't be long before she started hounding me about mine, and I wasn't in the mood for it any more than she was.

"Let's focus on what we should do next," Annie said, and I was more than willing to agree with her.

"If we're not going to tell Kathleen what we're planning to do, then we need to interview as many of our suspects as we can without arousing her suspicions."

"How do you propose we do that?"

"There's going to be a viewing tomorrow at the funeral home," I suggested. "I'm sure that everyone will be there."

"Pat, we can't wait until then. I'm willing to bet that if you make a few phone calls, you'll be able to find out where people are meeting this evening to offer their condolences."

"What are you going to be doing while I'm on the phone?" I asked her.

"I'm going to make cornbread and pineapple upside down cake," she replied. "We can't exactly show up empty handed, now, can we? Unless you want to bake. Then I'll make the phone calls."

"No, we should stick to what we're both best at," I conceded quickly. I could manage on a very basic level around the grill, but Annie was our chef, and what's more, everyone knew it.

I took one of the barstools at the counter and started making phone calls as Annie preheated one of the ovens and began mixing up her batters.

"Jack, this is Pat from the Iron."

"Pat, it's a sad day, isn't it?" Jack Forrester was a good customer as well as a longtime friend to us, as well as to Chester. Jack had retired from the Navy after putting in his twenty years, and then he'd worked for the state of North Carolina for another twenty, double-dipping pensions until he made more money on a monthly basis by not working a lick than nearly all of the rest of us did still slaving away. He was a year short of sixty, but he'd become firmly entrenched as the youngest member of the OTS—more formally known as the Old Timers' Society—a group of seniors, mostly men, who liked to pretend that they were capable of solving the world's ills, if only someone in power would ask them.

"It is sad indeed. I'm guessing folks are gathering somewhere this evening, and Annie and I would like to come by and offer our condolences."

"What a fright it must have been for you both finding him like that."

"More for Annie than me," I said, "not that it wasn't upsetting to me as well. Would you happen to know where everybody's getting together?"

"Lydia's hosting it, of course. Folks are already starting to gather at her place. From what I heard, Franklin didn't even offer, but there's no surprise there. The men shared a bloodline, but that was about all, and now they'll never be able to patch things up. Is Annie cooking up something special?" Was there a hint of food lust in his voice as he asked?

"As a matter of fact, she's making her famous cornbread and pineapple upside down cake."

"Not in the same recipe, I hope," Jack said with the hint of a smile in his voice that came through over the phone. "Sorry, that wasn't called for. After all, a man's dead. I'm heading over there right now myself, so I'll let them know that you're on your way."

"I'd appreciate it if you didn't say anything," I said hastily before he could hang up.

"Is there a reason you don't want anyone to know ahead of time?" Jack asked me suspiciously.

"It's just that I'm not entirely sure how Lydia and Franklin will take us showing up after what happened this morning, so I'd rather not give them time to dwell on it before we get there."

"Nobody blames the pair of you for what happened to the man," Jack said, slightly scolding me. "It was bad luck, and bad luck alone, that the two of you found him. Everyone in town knows how fond Chester was of both of you."

"Funny, but he never told either one of us that while he was still alive."

"Isn't that the way of the world? Most folks are uncomfortable heaping praise on their friends, but I've never been one of them. You and your sister are beloved in our little town, and we should tell you that more often than we probably do."

"Thanks, Jack. We'll see you over there."

"Until then," he said, and then the connection was broken.

Annie was just sliding two different cast iron skillets into the oven. "What did he say?"

"For starters, he wants to eat whatever you're willing to bring," I said.

"Jack has had a fondness for my food since he moved to town," she said with a partial smile. "I was talking about the get-together tonight."

"It's at Lydia's place, and according to Jack, it's already started," I said.

"Of course it has," Annie replied. "She wouldn't want Franklin upstaging her. Who knows? Someone with money might show up. I hear that she's always on the lookout for husband number four."

"Take it easy on her," I chided my sister. "After all, she just lost a brother."

"I'm fully aware of that fact, but we can't forget that she is still one of our suspects, Pat," Annie reminded me. "I feel everyone's pain, and I realize that only one of our suspects was

71

the one who actually killed Chester, but I can't be soft on any of them until we know for sure. This is going to be harder than I first thought. How are we going to grill these people without arousing their suspicions about our motives?"

I thought about the question for a few moments before I spoke. "We can't just ask questions and demand answers like Kathleen does. We have no official status in the case, but that doesn't mean that we can't hold different conversations with each of our suspects, and if our questions happen to be important to our investigation, then so much the better."

"What do we need to ask each of them, then?"

"Tell you what. We've got time while the cornbread and cake are baking," I said as I pulled out a sheet of paper and a pen I'd tucked into my pocket earlier to write our list of suspects down on. "Let's make a list."

⊷⟶◁✕▷⟵⊶

By the time the food was out of the oven and on cooling racks, we were ready to approach our suspects. While we'd been waiting for both items to bake, we'd written down a series of questions, and while I wanted to know the answers to each of them from everyone we were about to speak with, I had no idea how I was going to go about it. The questions, in no particular order, were as follows:

When was the last time you saw Chester alive?

Where were you at the time of the murder (in other words, what's your alibi)?

What kind of car do you drive?

Do you own any firearms?

When was the last time you were in the Iron (to account for stealing Annie's cast iron)?

Easier said than done, but we had to at least try.

———◦◇◦———

Finally, Annie judged her baked goods cool enough to transport, so she put them in containers with built-in covers we normally used for to-go orders, and we were on our way to Lydia's place in my Toyota Tundra pickup truck. Annie had wanted to take her Subaru Forester, but she was low on gas, so the driving was up to me while she held the fruits of her labor on her lap. There were a great many cars parked in front of Lydia's place by the time we got there, and I had to park the truck halfway down the block. I left myself plenty of room to give us a quick escape, just in case someone resented the hard questions my sister and I were about to ask.

———◦◇◦———

"How should we go about this?" I asked Annie before we reached the front steps of the mansion where Lydia was currently residing. I'd heard that she'd gotten it in her third and last divorce, though I doubted very much that it was going to be her final one. She'd moved up each time she'd married, always reaching for just a little bit more than she already had.

"I thought we'd just ask our questions and go," my sister replied.

"I don't think anyone's going to stand for us just grilling them. We have to work our questions into the conversation. Ideally, no one will even realize that they are being interrogated."

"I like that idea in theory, but I'm not sure how we're going to go about it in practice. I've got the feeling that whoever we speak with is going to feel as though we're ganging up on them."

"I'd be lying if I said I hadn't been thinking the same thing, too," I told her. It was the central flaw to our plan that I'd recognized myself, but I didn't like the only way there was to correct it, so I'd kept shoving it down into my thoughts.

Ultimately, though, I didn't see any other way to handle things, so it was time to bite the bullet and say aloud what both of us were thinking. "Annie, what do you think about the idea of us splitting up once we're inside? Not only can we cover more ground quicker, but we can also alleviate the issue of folks feeling that it's two against one."

"I really don't see that we have any choice," Annie answered. "As much as I love you, little brother, you can really cramp my style sometimes."

"Are you ever going to let me forget what happened before our senior prom?" I asked. "I didn't realize you and Clark Jenkins were making out in the hall closet when I went to get my coat."

"That's not where we started," she protested, "but Clark heard footsteps, and he always was kind of skittish."

"It's time to let that one go, Sis," I said.

"Fair enough. Not another word."

I couldn't believe what I was hearing. "Do you mean that?"

"Of course not," she said with the hint of a laugh in her voice. "Now, how should we divide our victims up? Strike that. I didn't mean that the way it must have sounded."

"I know that," I said. "How about if you take the men, and I'll handle the women?" This was exactly what I *didn't* want to happen, but I knew Annie well enough to realize that she'd never take my first suggestion, if out of sheer spite if nothing else.

"Okay, that sounds fine by me," she said, shocking me enough to make me nearly drop the cornbread, which I'd been ordered to carry while she transported the cake.

"Seriously? You're picking *this* moment to go along with my suggestion?"

Annie laughed. "Don't try to play me, Patrick. If you want the men, you need to ask for them."

"No, I'll gladly take three of our suspects over having just two. That dramatically improves my odds of trapping the killer myself."

Clearly she hadn't considered that possibility. To be honest, neither had I. "You know, you're right," Annie said. "The guys will probably be more willing to share with you than they will with me, and I know for a fact that the women aren't going to talk to you without being able to resist the temptation to bat their eyes at you."

"Don't be ridiculous," I said, feeling my cheeks heat slightly from blushing. "You're just trying to grab the lion's share of our suspects for yourself."

"True, but it's still a better plan than the one you suggested," she said with a smile.

I knew to give up when I was ahead. "Agreed. You take the women, I'll take the men, and we'll compare notes afterwards."

"It's a deal," Annie said just as we reached the wide veranda that served as a front porch for the McMansion. I was wondering how I was going to juggle the cornbread and knock on the door at the same time when I was saved from my dilemma. Lydia herself opened the door for us, and from her black shoes and dress to the hat with a veil pulled over her face, I realized that she was playing the grieving sister to the hilt.

"Our condolences for your loss," Annie said to her.

"How tragic for you to be the one who found him," Lydia replied. "Did he say anything before he died?"

Had she lost her mind? Chester had been long gone by the time Annie discovered his body on our front porch. "I thought you knew. He'd already been gone for some time when we found him," I said.

"Of course. I knew that. You'll have to excuse me. I don't know where my mind is. It was such a blow losing my dear brother like that."

"I'm sure that it was," Annie said as she handed me the

pineapple upside down cake, which I placed delicately on top of the cornbread. "Pat, won't you take those inside? I'd like a word with Lydia before I join you."

"Of course," I said. Annie was getting down to business, and it was time that I did so as well. I left them on the front porch together and made my way into the kitchen. Fortunately, one of the men on my list was lurking there. He already had a plate stacked high with food, so I could see that the murder hadn't thrown him off his feed, at any rate.

"Franklin, we're all so sorry for your loss," I said as I handed the food over to one of the women from the Ladies' Floral Society. Their group's responsibilities went far beyond horticulture, extending to bake sales to charities to wakes, always there ready and willing to lend a hand. Beatrice Masterson took the offered goods and, in a somber voice, said, "Annie's donations are always welcome."

"I'll tell her you said so," I said, and then I turned back to Franklin. He was clearly older than Chester had been, and the years had not been so kind to him. Whereas his younger brother had kept his boyish good looks, the older brother of the pair definitely showed his age. "When did you hear about what happened to your brother?" I asked him.

"Lydia called me at home. I was still asleep. Pretty awful way to wake up, if you ask me."

I wanted to ask him if he'd been alone at the time, but I didn't know how to word it without infuriating the man. For the moment, I was just going to assume that the twice-divorced man had been alone. "When was the last time you saw him?"

Franklin looked up from some questionable-looking ham loaf. "We chatted for a minute the other day on the phone, but I hadn't seen him in days. Pity, that. I would have liked to have had the chance to say good-bye."

"I'm sure he would have enjoyed that as well," I said. What

was that supposed to mean? I was struggling with fitting my questions into the conversation, and it was clear that I had a lot to learn about interrogating suspects. If the statement sounded awkward to Franklin, he didn't show it. I followed up with, "Didn't I see you at the Iron yesterday?"

"No, it wasn't me. I wasn't there," Franklin said curtly.

"Are you sure? I could swear that I saw you. You're still driving that green Cadillac, aren't you?"

"I drive a dark blue Suburban," he corrected me as he shook his head, "and I'm sure I wouldn't forget coming by your little general store."

I didn't know if he was telling the truth or not about visiting the Iron, but at least his vehicle description matched the information Chester had provided. How did he get Annie's pan, though, if he wasn't at the grill at some point? I'd have to dig a little more into that. I had one more question for him, but I didn't have a clue about how to bring it up. I was running out of time, too. I saw Grady of pennysaver fame heading in our direction. "Maybe you can give me some advice. I'm looking to purchase a rifle. Do you have any ideas what kind I should buy?"

Franklin stared at me for a moment as though I'd suddenly grown a third eye. "Sorry, I can't help you." As Grady approached us, Franklin said, "I need to see about something in back. Thanks for coming."

And then he was gone in a flash. Grady looked disappointed as he joined me. "Where is he off to in such a hurry? I wanted to interview him for my special edition."

"Good luck with that," I said with a grin I didn't feel as I sidestepped him and went off in search of my own quarry.

The problem was that I had too much immediate success.

Two of our suspects were deep in conversation with each other! I couldn't wait to get Bryson alone, so I dove in headfirst, butting my way into his talk with Julia Crane.

"Tragic, isn't it?" I asked them, interrupting their whispered exchange as I approached them.

"We were just saying the exact same thing," Bryson said. "What a loss to the community," he added.

"It's okay to admit that you two had issues when he was alive," Julia said softly as she touched her beau's arm. "The fact that you'd come here this afternoon says a lot about how you feel about me."

"It's not much, but standing by you is all that I can do right now," he answered. Bryson was extremely solicitous when he spoke to her, giving her every ounce of his attention. Was that his secret for attracting women despite his outward appearance? I decided to forget about that particular conundrum. It was time to start asking questions, even if it meant grilling them both at the same time. I already knew that they'd both been at the Iron the day before when the skillet had been stolen, so thankfully, that was one question I didn't need to work into the conversation. "I was just speaking with Grady Simpson," I said, which was the entire truth, but the lie I was about to add was not. "We were talking about the last time that we saw Chester. I think he's going to publish some kind of memorial in his paper."

"Leave it to Grady to try to make a dollar out of someone else's misery," Bryson said with disdain.

"I don't know. I think it's sweet," Julia countered. "Chester and I had our differences lately, but once upon a time, we were in love, and that's something that I'll never forget."

I suddenly realized that they'd both neatly sidestepped the question. How could I get them to answer it now? In an instant, I decided that there was nothing like the direct approach. "I spoke with him yesterday at the Iron myself," I said, getting the ball rolling. "How about you two?"

"We spoke yesterday as well," Bryson admitted. "It was brief, and a bit heated, to be honest with you, but that was the nature of our relationship. He recently beat me out on a land deal that I'd been working on for two months, and frankly, he was gloating about it a bit."

"I wouldn't take it too personally, Bryson. Chester always did enjoy teasing you," Julia said.

"When did you see him last?" I asked her.

She frowned for a moment in thought before she spoke. "It must have been several days ago. I can't remember the details, but I do wish that I'd been kinder to him now."

"Don't beat yourself up over it," Bryson said, speaking in a calm and soothing manner. "There was no way to know that it would be the last time you two spoke."

"Thank you," she said, clearly appreciating his words of comfort.

At least they were answering my questions. It was time to push a little harder for more information. "Where were you when it happened?" I asked them both as innocently as I could muster. Was it possible that they were about to alibi each other?

"What an odd question to ask us," Julia said as she looked at me suspiciously. "Pat, why on earth would you want to know that?"

It was a fair question and, worse yet, one that I didn't happen to have a ready answer for. Fortunately, Bryson stepped in and saved me. "Julia, don't forget that Pat was upstairs when Chester was being murdered just below him. I don't blame him one bit for asking."

I nodded my thanks to Bryson and decided to run with his excuse. "To be honest with you, it's helping me cope with what happened by asking other people where they were."

Bryson put a hand on my shoulder and turned his charm straight at me. "I understand completely. My whereabouts are easy enough to explain. I was in Glory Landing having breakfast with Nathan Pepper. I've been trying to buy some land from him for ages so I can develop it, and he insisted that I be there before the sun came up. I had to push my Escalade to its limit to get there in time."

Score! I'd gotten the answers to two questions with one inquiry. I knew it was just beginner's luck, but I wasn't going to take it for granted.

We both looked expectantly at Julia. Finally, she shrugged as she said, "It's nowhere near as interesting as your early-morning meeting. I was home in bed, fast asleep."

Now all I had to do was ask them about firearms. Even in our part of the South, it wasn't all that easy a subject to bring up. Then I had an idea. "I've been thinking about buying some protection for the Iron after this happened. Do either one of you happen to know anything about guns?"

"I used to go hunting with my father when I was a little girl," Julia said, surprisingly. "Trust me, I got out of that just as soon as I could manage it without hurting his feelings. He'd always wanted a son, and until I put my foot down, he tried his best to turn me into one."

"I'm awfully glad that he failed," Bryson said to her with a smile before he added, "I had a twenty-two rifle growing up, just like all of my friends did, but I put it away a long time ago. I just didn't enjoy shooting tin cans after a while, you know?"

So both of them knew their way around firearms. All I had left on my list to ask was what Julia drove, but it appeared that I wasn't going to get the chance.

My sister called my name out from across the room.

I put up my index finger in her direction, signaling that I'd need another minute, but she was insistent.

"You'd better go see what's happening," Bryson said. "It appears to be urgent."

"No worries. I'm sure that it can wait," I replied.

"I've seen that look on enough faces to know that it probably can't," he countered. "Go on. It was nice chatting with you again."

"If you'll excuse me," I said, knowing that there was no way I could postpone speaking with Annie now, "I'll be back with you both in a minute."

"Don't come back on my account," Bryson said. "Unfortunately, I can't stay." He glanced at his watch, and then he turned to Julia. "Sorry, but duty calls."

"No worries. I'll see you tonight," she said. It was interesting that there was no physical contact between them, but seeing how it was her ex-husband's farewell, I supposed that it was perfectly understandable.

"Did you two come together, by any chance?" I asked them. "I could always give you a ride home later, Julia."

"No, I brought my own car, since I knew that Bryson would be skipping out early."

"You drive a cute little convertible, don't you?" I asked.

"I used to, but I switched over to one of those SUV monsters last month. I'm having a change of heart, though, so I'll be going back to something fast and small soon. I can't believe how much gas those things take, and parking is a nightmare."

I was about to ask her what color it was when Annie grabbed my arm, and from the tension she was applying, she wasn't about to let go.

"Nice seeing you both," I said as my sister dragged me away.

Whatever she had to say had better be urgent.

I wasn't a fan of being muscled around, especially by one of my sisters.

This had better be good.

CHAPTER 12: ANNIE

"**O**KAY, YOU'VE GOT MY ATTENTION. What's so important?" Pat asked me as I kept my fingers clenched around his upper arm and drug him away from Bryson and Julia.

"She was on my list, and you know it," I said. "Why were you talking to her just now?"

"Julia was standing there with Bryson," he said. "What was I supposed to do, ask her to leave?"

"You might have, but clearly you didn't. Did you grill her as well?" I already knew the answer to that question. I'd finished with Lydia earlier, and as far as I could see, Harper wasn't there yet, if she was even coming at all.

"Some of the questions on our list might have come up," he reluctantly admitted. "Annie, I didn't do it on purpose."

I eased up on my twin brother's arm. I shouldn't have vented my frustrations on him. Lydia had blown me off completely, and I'd looked in vain for my other two objects of interest without success until I'd found my brother interrogating one of them.

"What did you find out?" I asked him, calming down a little as I spoke.

"Do you really want to do this here and now?" my brother asked me softly. "As far as I'm concerned, it can wait until you're finished with your interrogations. If you are, then we can leave."

"I haven't had any luck at all," I said, letting my frustration spill out a little.

Pat grinned at me, which was exactly the wrong way to react to what I'd just told him. "Do you need a hand, Sis?"

"Not on your life," I said firmly. "But if you're finished, you're free to leave. Don't worry about me. I'll find a way back to my car."

Pat knew that he'd crossed a line, and he began to apologize immediately. That was one of the things that I loved most about my twin, his willingness to say that he was sorry with the least hint of provocation. "I'm sorry, Annie. I shouldn't have said that. I was wrong. Now tell me, what can I do to make it up to you?"

"For starters, you can help me find Harper," I said.

"I thought I saw her heading to the back porch a few minutes ago," he said.

"Seriously? You haven't spoken with her, too, have you?"

"No, ma'am. Scout's honor. She's all yours."

"Then you need to stay right here," I said as I put a hand on Pat's chest. "I'll be right back."

"Don't worry about me. I'm going to go get some pineapple upside down cake."

"You can get that any time you want it," I said as I brushed past him on my way to the porch.

He grinned at me. "I know, and I want some right now. Good luck."

"Thanks," I said as I hurried out the back door. I needed to speak with Harper, and after I was finished with her, it was going to be time to take another run at Lydia. She might have won the battle earlier, but I wasn't about to concede the war.

But Harper was first.

＊＜◇＞＊

She was alone, thank goodness. I didn't know how Pat had managed to deal with two suspects at once, not that I wasn't a multitasker in most of the things I did in life. It wasn't anything especially taxing for me to be running a dozen breakfast or lunch orders at the same time, but that was when I was behind the counter and at my most comfortable.

Harper was an attractive woman, and it wasn't hard to see why Chester had been attracted to her. If I had to guess, I'd say that she tipped the scales somewhere around one hundred forty pounds—somewhere close to my weight—but she was at least six inches taller than I was. Probably the most distinctive thing about her was her jet-black hair, and she had a lot of it. Where a great many women were opting for shorter cuts these days, Harper's hair nearly reached her waist.

When I came upon her, she had obviously been crying, and the moment I opened the back door, she tried to hide the fact with her hand. "I'm sorry. I promised myself that I wasn't going to cry, but I couldn't stand being in there with Franklin and Lydia for one more second. To hear them tell it, they were Chester's closest confidants. I knew better, but I couldn't say anything, so I had to leave before I spoke my mind."

"I'm so sorry for your loss," I said, and this time, there was nothing automatic about it. It must be tragic losing someone you loved in such a violent way, and my first thoughts were of sympathy for her, but I couldn't give in to those. After all, Harper might have been the one who'd done it, and if that was the case, she didn't deserve my sympathy at all.

Harper nodded her thanks, and then she took her hands in mine. "Annie, I'm sorry that you had to be the one to find him. It must have been terrible for you."

"I've had better mornings," I admitted. "Were you at least on good terms with Chester when he died? I understand the two of you had a rather volatile relationship." Now was the time to see if she'd tell me the truth about her confrontation with Chester the night before he died. Les Hodges had seen the two of them fighting in the park on the eve of Chester's murder, but would Harper admit to it?

"It's just awful," Harper said as she started to cry again. "We had a stupid argument last night, and I never got the opportunity to tell him that I was sorry and to make up with him. Now I'll have to live with that for the rest of my life."

As sympathetically as I could manage, I asked, "What exactly were you fighting about?"

"He wanted more from me than I was ready to give," she confessed in a near whisper.

"In what way?" I might be pushing her too hard, but I honestly wanted to know. After all, it might just have a bearing on what had happened to the man.

"I'm sorry. It's too painful to talk about," she answered. It was an excellent evasion, and I knew that particular bit of curiosity was going to have to go unsatisfied, at least for the moment.

"Let's talk about something else," I said brightly. "Didn't I see you at the Iron yesterday afternoon?"

She nodded. "I came by to check my mail. I've been waiting for a letter from my uncle. He's so old fashioned that he never uses email. In fact, I'm not entirely certain that he even owns a computer." So at least she admitted being near where I stored the skillet that had been used as a murder weapon.

"Did it arrive?"

"No, I'll have to check again tomorrow, not that I'm certain that I can ever step foot inside the Iron again after what happened to Chester there."

"I know how you feel, but don't blame the Iron for it. It could have happened anywhere."

"Who would have done such a thing?" Harper asked me, the despair heavy in her voice.

"I wish I knew," I said truthfully. "How did you find out about it?"

"As a matter of fact, your sister called me," she said, tearing up again. "I'd been awake half the night trying to sleep after the argument I'd had with Chester, but I'd finally managed to nod off when she called to tell me what had happened."

There was no way to confirm that, so it was just one more dead end in the line of questioning Pat and I had agreed on ahead of time.

"There you are," Lydia said as she stormed out onto the porch and found us talking. "People are asking about you." Almost as an afterthought, she acknowledged my presence. "You understand, don't you, Annie?"

"Of course," I said.

Harper frowned at her late boyfriend's sister, and then she started to hurry down the porch steps, away from the house and the people inside it.

"Where do you think you are going?" Lydia demanded.

"I can't stay here one minute longer," Harper said, the tears now heavily flowing.

I craned my neck to see what kind of car she was going to drive away in, but she vanished around the house before I could manage it.

"I warned Chester from the start that girl was overdramatic," Lydia said flatly. It was odd to see how satisfied she looked concerning Harper's departure. Did it just mean there would be more attention in her direction, or did she have another, darker reason to be happy about the situation?

"They were getting quite close, weren't they?" I asked.

"Is that what she told you? Chester was getting ready to dump her. He told me so himself." Wow, I doubted that I'd ever been that smug in my life.

Could that be true? "When did this happen?"

"He was going to cut her loose last night," Lydia said.

"Did he go through with it?"

"I assumed that it was as good as done after what he told me yesterday afternoon when he came by to see me. When she showed up here this afternoon like some kind of grieving widow, I began to have my doubts. Either that, or he did as he'd promised and dumped her, but she's here angling for an inheritance of some sort anyway."

"They hadn't been together that long," I said. "Would Chester have actually rewritten his will in her favor after such a short courtship?" Chester had mentioned leaving ten percent of his accumulated wealth to Harper in the letter he'd written us, but I was wondering if anyone else knew about it, in particular either one of his siblings.

"Who knows? My brother was unpredictable in his best moments, so who can say for sure one way or the other? He had an attorney he used for such things, but I haven't seen hide nor hair of him since what happened to poor Chester."

"I've met him. He came by the Iron earlier," I blurted out without thinking about the ramifications of telling her.

"Why on earth would he visit you before he sought me out?" she asked me as she tried to burn holes into me with her stare.

"He wanted directions," I said lamely. I didn't believe it, and I was certain that Lydia didn't, either. It was time to change the subject. "Was that your black Expedition I saw parked out front?"

"Yes, it's a ghastly beast to drive. I'm going to trade it in for something more practical as soon as I get the chance. I never should have let Chester talk me into getting it in the first place."

"Why did he care what you drove?" I asked.

"Chester liked to butt his nose where it didn't belong. Is it any wonder how he met his end?" For one moment, she'd dropped the grieving sister routine and had let her true view of her brother slip. In an effort to salvage what she could, she quickly added, "Everything he did was out of concern for his fellow man, but not everyone accepted him for the way that he was."

"Were you here when you heard the news?" I asked her, struggling to get another question in before something pulled her away.

"Actually, I was driving back from Charlotte. I spent the night there with friends, and I was making an early start of it returning home. I was so overcome with grief that I had to pull over when I heard the news."

That was an interesting twist. I decided to get in one more question as quickly as I could, and I knew that I had to make it a good one. Should I ask her about firearms, or about her presence at the Iron the day before? Unfortunately, I didn't have time to ask her either question. The back door opened, and Franklin stuck his head out, clearly irritated about something. "I thought you came out here to fetch Harper, but when I looked out the window, I saw her driving away in that ridiculous little fire-engine-red Miata of hers." Without realizing it, Franklin had just answered one of the questions I'd failed to get answered by Harper.

"She said she couldn't stay one second longer," Lydia answered dryly.

"Why would she act that way? Lydia, what did you say to her?" Franklin asked, his features growing angry upon hearing the news.

"Me? Nothing, I was the perfect hostess. If you don't believe me, you can ask Annie. She was standing right here the entire time."

I nodded. "Harper was overwhelmed by everything, and she told us that she needed to go."

Lydia offered me a brief smile for corroborating her story, but there was no warmth in it.

Franklin took that in, and then he must have decided not to

argue the point. "You need to get in there, Sis. There are folks who came by to pay their respects, and evidently I'm not good enough. They're asking for you."

Lydia did her best to hide her smile that time, but I still managed to catch it. She turned to me and said, "Excuse me, Annie, but I must see to this onerous task."

Funny, but she didn't look as though she minded at all. "Of course," I said. I was about to ask Franklin why he hadn't been happy about Lydia's responses to Harper, but I never got the chance. As Lydia reached the door, she turned to her last living brother. "Don't tarry. You need to be there with me as well."

"Coming," he said in a grumble, and suddenly I was left alone.

Not for long, though.

Pat came out twenty seconds later, smiling softly.

"What's so funny?" I asked him.

"You managed to get your suspects to come to you, didn't you? Please tell me that you learned something that's going to help us in our investigation."

"I will if you will," I acknowledged. "I've gotten all that I'm going to get today. We should go somewhere and compare notes."

"That's a great idea. Why don't we use my apartment above the store," he suggested.

"My place is closer," I said. Pat liked my cabin in the woods just fine, but at heart he was a city mouse through and through. "Don't worry, it won't be dark for hours, and everybody knows that's when the bears, the wolves, and the deranged lunatics all come out to play."

"You think you're funny, but you're really not," Pat said.

"Come on, you haven't seen my place since I got my new curtains," I suggested.

"Well, I can't very well miss that, can I?" he asked. "Fine, we'll go to the cabin, but I'm telling you right now, I'm going to be out of there by dark, no matter what you say."

"It's a good thing it's summer, then," I said with a smile. "Otherwise it would already be dark. Come on. It will give you a chance to drive that truck of yours down a real country road instead of on the city streets you are used to."

"I do like doing that," he admitted.

"We can even throw a bale of hay in back if you want so you can look like a real cowboy," I suggested.

"Thanks, but I don't want to have to wash the bed out to get all of the straw out."

I knew better than to laugh, but I couldn't help myself. I reined it in after a second, though, and my twin graciously decided not to notice.

We didn't get the chance to make a clean getaway, though.

Our sister, still dressed in her sheriff's uniform, was sitting on the tailgate of Pat's truck when we got there, and from the look of things, she wasn't happy about being kept waiting.

The problem with that was that we hadn't been expecting to see her; at least, I hadn't.

"Did you know that she'd be waiting for us?" I asked Pat as we neared Kathleen.

"It's news to me. How about you?"

"I'm just as deep in the dark as you are."

"Then let's see what she has to say," Pat said, and then, in a near whisper, he added, "Remember, mum's the word about what we're doing."

"Right back at you," I replied.

"Hey, Sis," I said the moment we made eye contact. "Were we supposed to meet you here?"

"For some funny reason, I thought we'd be going to pay our respects as a family," she admitted.

"Sorry, but we brought fresh cornbread and pineapple upside down cake, and we wanted to get them here while they were still warm."

"Why do you think I wanted to come with you?" she asked with the hint of a smile. "Now I'll look like I didn't care enough to bring them anything and that I'm just there to try to solve Chester's murder."

"Would that be so far from the truth?" Pat asked her.

"Probably not, but I wanted to at least look neighborly while I was doing it. Next time something like this happens, give me a call before you two decide to go without me, okay?"

"We will, but I sincerely hope that it never happens again," I said quickly before Pat could answer.

"But if it does, you'll be our first call," my twin chimed in.

"What's it like in there?" she asked, clearly hesitant about getting our impressions, though it was just as obvious that she was dying to know.

"It's pretty dreary, actually," I answered. "Wouldn't you say so, Pat?"

My idiot brother nodded, and then he echoed one word from my description. "Dreary."

Kathleen looked at him strangely, and then she glanced at me. "What's up with him?"

"He's been eating my pineapple upside down cake," I said. "You know how weird he gets when he's hopped up on sugar. For him, it should be listed as a controlled substance."

"Hey, I'm not that bad," Pat protested, but Kathleen and I both just grinned at him. In a few seconds, he conceded, "Okay, maybe you're both right, but that stuff has always been dangerous around me."

"Well, wish me luck," Kathleen said as she got off Pat's lowered tailgate.

She was two steps away when Pat asked, "Wouldn't 'happy hunting' be more appropriate?"

Kathleen turned to look at him. "Is that really called for?"

"Like I said, ignore him. It's just the sugar talking," I said.

Kathleen shrugged for a moment, and then she headed for the front door.

Once she was out of earshot, I asked my twin, "What was that about?"

"You told me to play it low key."

"Not comatose, though," I protested. "No more monosyllabic answers, okay?"

"Make up your mind, Annie. You either get the life of the party, or the mysterious loner. There's no happy medium for me."

"Fortunately our older sister knows that as well as I do," I answered. "Pat, if we're going to keep lying to Kathleen, even if they are all going to be sins of omission, you're going to need to get better at it, and fast, too."

"You're not so great, either," he mumbled in protest.

"Maybe not, but at least I'm better than you," I replied, and then I chuckled to ease the sting of what I'd just said to him. "Let's go compare notes."

"Sounds like a plan to me," Pat said, and he started driving in the direction of my home in the woods.

CHAPTER 13: PAT

"HEY, YOU MIGHT WANT TO slow down a little. You're going to ding up your precious truck if you're not careful," Annie said with a grin as I tried to navigate the bumpy and unpredictable road that led from the main highway to her cabin in the woods.

"You need somebody to deliver more gravel out here," I said as my truck bounced around a little on the rough path to her place. The driveway, if you cared to call it that, led up a steep incline, and part of the passageway edged narrowly close to a dropoff that I would hate to be forced off of.

"I don't have any problem with it," she said. "You just have to know how to drive it, that's all."

"Are you trying to discourage anyone from visiting you all the way out here in the middle of nowhere, Annie?" I asked her as I avoided another patch of bad road. At least I could see her cabin in the distance, nestled by a lake that our great grandfather had commissioned to be built when he'd first come to the area. My sister's place looked safe and snug in the distance to me, but I wasn't about to stay until dark. There was no way that I was going to risk driving this obscenity called a road in the dark without a navigator.

"It's worked fine so far," she admitted. "Pat, we see people all day long, six days a week at the Iron. When I come out here, I'm pretty certain that I'm going to be left alone, and that's the way that I like it."

"I'm beginning to see why no men have attempted to take you out lately," I said as I hit another rough spot. I drove a pickup, and I was nervous about the driveway; what chance did a potential suitor have if he owned a more reasonable vehicle for the twenty-first century?

"If the road to my cabin is enough to ease a man's ardor, then he isn't the right guy for me, anyway," she said. I had to admit that she had a point. My sister made no bones about her lifestyle choices, and anyone who wanted to date her had to pass this gauntlet and more before getting the chance.

We made it at last, and I pulled into a spot of trampled grass in front of her place. I shut off the engine, and then I asked her, "You don't have your car here, so you're going to have to drive back on that road in the dark after I take you back to the Iron. Are you certain that this was a good idea?"

"Don't worry about me. I could drive that lane blindfolded," she said.

"Do me a favor and never ever prove that to me, okay?" I felt like kissing the ground when I got out of my truck.

"You've got to admit that it's worth a few frayed nerves for that view," Annie said as she pointed to the vista.

I took in the cabin's rustic, Adirondack-style exterior, the trees surrounding it, and the lake just a few dozen feet from her doorstep. In town, it hadn't looked as though the sun was anywhere close to setting, but out here, where the mountains formed boundaries that reached well up into the sky, it appeared to be much later than my watch proclaimed. Annie must have caught me glancing at the time. "Don't worry, Pat. It's a lot easier driving down the hill than it was coming up." She looked back at her surroundings once more, and then she let out her most contented sigh.

"You really do love it up here, don't you?"

"What's not to love? My nearest neighbors are deer, rabbits, ducks, and squirrels. The great outdoors is a constantly changing scene that is vastly more entertaining that anything television could ever offer. I have my solar panels to give me all the power I ever need, a fully stocked wood shed to keep me warm and cook my food, and an outhouse that is perfectly suitable for my needs. I don't pay for water or electricity, and I've never had to call a handyman since I've lived out here by myself."

"You would have been perfect for life a few centuries ago," I said. "Don't you long for modern conveniences, Annie?"

"No thanks. My life suits me just fine," she said. "Let's go inside. I made some cookies you're going to love."

"Oatmeal raisin?" I asked hopefully. They were my favorite, and Annie knew that better than anyone else in the world.

"Would I dare offer you any other kind?" she asked me with a grin.

"How did you bake them in that wood-fired monstrosity of an oven?" I asked her as we headed for the front door.

"My oven here works great, but I don't do much baking in the heat of summer. I made these back at the Iron," she said as she patted her oversized purse.

"Are you telling me that you've had them all along and are just now offering them to me?" I asked as I reached out for the goodies.

"I was holding them back in case I needed an extra incentive to get you to come out to my place," she said lightly as she offered me the small Tupperware container.

I popped the lid off and took a deep breath. The four cookies housed inside smelled like Eden to me, with hints of cinnamon and nutmeg mixed in with the baked oats, raisins, and dough. I took a bite of the first cookie, and then I embraced the explosion of flavor I experienced. "Now all I need is a glass of cold milk, and I can die a happy man."

"My fridge has some chilling just for you," she said as she

took her key and unlocked the front door. When folks heard that my sister lived in a cabin, they usually assumed that it was made from logs, not studs cut from them. The original cabin at this location had been made of spruce logs indeed, cut and dried on the property, but a devastating lightning strike had reduced the entire place to a pile of scorched rubble. Our mom and dad had undertaken to rebuild on the same site—having my twin sister's love for the outdoors in equal portions to hers—but they chose conventional framing this time around. The cabin was twelve feet by sixteen and offered everything that Annie needed. There was an open area as we walked in sporting a small living space filled with a couch and two chairs. There wasn't exactly any room inside for any dividers, so her kitchen and shower segued from that space, with the ceiling of that section lower to accommodate the sleeping loft above. Annie's wood-burning stove offered a single heat source for the entire interior that also supplied the hot water for dishes as well as heating a jug full of water for her shower. It also provided a cooking surface on top, as well as an oven beside the firebox. To top things off, the door where the firewood went was partially made of glass, offering her a nice view of the flames as they burned. It hadn't been cheap, and it weighed a ton, but it had been worth it. Her shower and sink were walled off into a small enclosed space, and a ladder led to the top of the loft, an area that would have made me claustrophobic to sleep in despite the skylight just over her pillow. Downstairs, full front and back porches bracketed her living space to complete her home. I had more room in my loft apartment than she had in the entire footprint of her place, but neither one of us would have traded what we had for the life the other one led.

"I like the new curtains," I said just before popping another cookie into my mouth. I was spoiling my appetite for dinner, but I didn't care. Annie's cookies were a rare treat for me, and that was probably a good thing. Otherwise I'd weigh eight hundred pounds and never make it up the stairs to my own place back in town.

"Thanks. I was thinking of you when I made them."

"You are truly a multitalented woman," I said with pride in my twin.

"You're not so bad yourself," she said as she offered the promised milk.

I took a sip, thought about eating another cookie, and then I realized that I shouldn't. "Are these all for me, or did you want one?" I asked her as I held the container in a protective gesture.

She laughed. "You don't have to share them with anyone if you don't want to."

"I suppose you could have one," I said grudgingly.

"I like them, but I couldn't be able to justify depriving you. Now, tell me what you learned at Lydia's house. I just hope you uncovered more than I was able to find out."

<hr>

By the time we were finished compiling our lists into one long treatise, the daylight was definitely waning. As I stood, I said, "Come on, Annie. Let's head back to the Iron so we can get your car."

She glanced outside and frowned. "Pat, we have plenty of time before it gets really dark out."

"Maybe for you, but I'm not as comfortable driving that bad excuse for a road as you are."

"But I still want to talk about what we've come up with so far and where we go from here," Annie protested.

"We can talk all you want to on the drive back," I said as I headed for the door. "It's a shame you don't have some kind of porch light out front."

"Oh, really?" she asked in a voice that made me realize that she'd finally done something to combat one of my complaints about her place.

When we got outside, I saw an array of solar-powered landscaping lights illuminating the path from the door to what passed as her parking area. "Those are really pretty," I conceded.

"Wait until we get to your truck, and then turn around."

I did as she instructed, and when I pivoted, I saw that she'd put solar lights on the cabin as well. They traced the entire outline of the building's form, from the base of the porch up one side all the way to the roof crest and then back down again. As I watched them come on, they began to twinkle, providing a sight that would be suitable for anyone's Christmas card. "Isn't it a little late in the year for holiday lighting?" I asked her with a grin.

"I'd rather think of it as being early. It's pretty, isn't it?"

I took in the view as the sun began to set over the lake, sending out shoots of red, gold, and yellow into the evening sky. It was amazing. "I can see the appeal of it," I replied.

"But not for you, right?"

"Let's just say I enjoy visiting, but I wouldn't want to live here," I said. "Now come on. We don't have much time."

"Worrywart," she said as she stuck her tongue out at me playfully.

"That's me," I replied, trying my best, and failing, not to laugh.

"Okay, let's recap," Annie said as she started reading from the list we'd just compiled. I glanced over and looked at it for a second, but she quickly chided me. "Hey, I'll do the reading while you keep watching the road."

"Got it, boss," I said.

I'd stared at the list long enough while we'd been creating it that I really didn't need to see it to know what it said. Still, Annie went on to summarize what we'd found as I drove, carefully studying the perilous path in front of me, but all the while listening to what she had to say.

"Chester's brother, Franklin, is the first name on our list. He claims that he spoke with Chester over the phone a few days ago but hasn't seen him in weeks. If we can find someone to dispute that, we might be able to break him. His alibi was a call from his sister, but he could have taken that anywhere, so it doesn't do us much good. He drives a dark-blue Suburban, which might be mistaken for black in the darkness of early morning, he wouldn't admit to owning a gun when you pressed him, and finally, he claimed that he wasn't in the Iron all day yesterday. If either Skip or Edith remember seeing him, we might be able to use it against him. Hey, watch out for that turn. It's nasty in the dark."

"I'm being careful," I said as I overcorrected the truck's steering. "Keep reading."

"I'm trying, but it's getting a little tough to see," she admitted.

"There's a penlight in the glove box," I told her. "Try that."

She got out the small light I kept there for emergencies, flicked it on, and then she shined it on the page. "Much better. Okay, Bryson Oak is next. He's long been a rival to Chester in business and in love, and he's currently dating Chester's ex-wife, Julia. He said that he was in Glory Landing having breakfast with someone named Nathan Pepper, so we need to track him down and see if that's true. Bryson drives an Escalade, but we have no idea what color it is, so that's something we'll need to find out. He admits to shooting his twenty-two as a teenager but not in recent history. Maybe we should find out if any of our suspects has bought rifle ammo anytime lately?"

"Do you mean besides from us?" I asked as I jerked the wheel sharply to avoid a dark object that had suddenly appeared in front of me.

Annie dropped the penlight. "What happened?"

"I thought I saw something," I admitted.

When I didn't go on, she asked, "What was it, a deer, a raccoon, or maybe an alien? At least give me a hint, Pat."

"It was low to the ground, and its eyes reflected back at me when my headlights hit them," I said.

"I'm guessing that it was just a raccoon. Don't worry."

"I'm not worried," I said, loosening my death grip on the steering wheel.

Annie retrieved the light and turned her attention back to the list. "The last thing is that we know Bryson was at the Iron the day before the murder, so he could have swiped my pan."

"Read on."

"Harper Gentry is next. She was dating Chester when he died, and she admits that they fought the night before. Whether he was breaking up with her or it was something else, there was definitely conflict there. As for our other questions, she claims she was home asleep by herself, and she drives a bright red Miata, which we both know is a car that no one could ever mistake for a large SUV. On the other hand, she admitted to being at the Iron when the skillet was stolen, so maybe she borrowed someone else's car and used it to try to run Chester down."

I was nearly at the end of the drive and couldn't get there soon enough as far as I was concerned. Annie's voice had managed to serve as a distraction for me, and it helped hearing the facts laid out so succinctly.

"That just leaves us with Julia Crane and Lydia to discuss. Let's do Julia first. Does an ex-wife really need more of a motive for murder than that? We don't know when she saw Chester last or what she drives, but she admitted to going hunting as a little girl, and like most of the rest of our suspects, she claims that she was home alone sleeping at the time of the murder, and we know that she was at the Iron the day before. As for Lydia, if she thought she was going to inherit anything from her brother, she might have killed him out of pure greed. She claims that she saw Chester the afternoon before the murder, and that she was coming back from an overnight visit with friends in Charlotte when she heard the news about his demise."

"We need to follow up on that and see if she was really where she said that she was," I said as my tires hit solid pavement again.

"I'd love to, but I never got their names from her."

"Maybe we can press her a little harder about that and find out," I suggested as I made my way back to the Iron.

"Maybe. Anyway, as to the rest of our questions, Lydia drives a black Expedition, and I have no idea if she knows anything about firearms or if she was at the Iron the day before the murder." Annie frowned at our list. "We have quite a few incompletes on here, don't we?"

"I think we're doing extremely well, given our limitations," I said.

"How does Kathleen manage to do it?" Annie asked me.

"Well, for one thing, she has the advantage of having a badge and a gun," I countered.

"Maybe so," Annie answered. She was awfully quiet.

"Hey, are you okay?"

She just shrugged. "I guess it's all just starting to sink in. This time yesterday, Chester was alive and well, and now, less than twenty-four hours later, he's been dead for most of the day. You just never know, do you?"

I'd had a suspicion that it might take some time to sink in when my twin had first found Chester's body. "I've got an idea. Why don't you bunk with me at the Iron tonight? You can have my bedroom, and I'll take the couch. Shoot, sometimes I sleep out there anyway, so you won't be putting me out at all."

"Thanks for the offer, but if it's all the same to you, I think I'll head back to my cabin. It's really the only place where I feel at peace with the world, and I need that feeling tonight more than ever. You don't mind, do you?"

"Of course not. If you need me, I want you to promise me that you'll call, no matter what time it is. I'm ten minutes away, but if there's an emergency, I can do it in seven."

She grinned at me. "Even taking my horrific driveway into consideration?"

"Even then. I wouldn't brave that drive in the dark for anyone else, but for you, I'll make an exception."

"I'm telling Kathleen you said that."

"Annie, don't you suspect that she already knows?"

My twin hesitated before answering. "You're right. There's no need to add insult to injury."

We arrived at the Iron, and I parked my truck beside Annie's Subaru.

There was one problem, though.

Someone was parked on the other side of it, a person I wasn't all that excited about seeing.

⁂

As Annie and I got out of the truck, Molly got out of her car as well and joined us.

"Hi, Molly," Annie said, and then she glanced at me. "Aren't you going to say hello, Pat?"

"What brings you by this time of night?" I asked her instead.

Before she could answer, Annie cut in. "No, try again, Patrick."

"It's okay," Molly said, but my twin wouldn't allow it.

"Thanks for saying that, but I'm trying to housebreak him, so he needs to learn to be cordial."

"I'm not a puppy in need of training," I protested.

"That remains to be seen," Annie said.

I decided to take the path of least resistance. "Hi, Molly. You look good." As a matter of fact, she looked beautiful to me, gorgeous beyond all description, but I couldn't bring myself to tell her that.

"Thanks," she said as she blushed a little. "Pat, I hate to just barge in unannounced, but do you have a second?"

I didn't even get a chance to answer before my sister spoke up.

"I was just leaving," Annie said as she kissed my cheek, and then she whispered in my ear, "Don't blow this, Pat!"

"Call me when you get home," I told her, pretending to ignore her earnest advice.

"Sure thing."

Without another word, Annie got into her car and drove off, leaving Molly and me standing there alone in the moonlight.

"Would you like to come up?" I suggested, never dreaming for a second that she'd agree. Since we'd broken up the last time, we hadn't spent much time together, and none of it had been alone.

"That would be nice," she answered, surprising me.

As I unlocked the side door of the Iron for us, I couldn't help wondering what had brought her here and what was so urgent that it couldn't wait until morning.

It looked as though I was about to find out, though.

CHAPTER 14: ANNIE

I WISHED THAT PAT COULD HAVE seen his own expression when he realized that Molly was there at the Iron waiting for us. That boy was smitten like I'd never seen him with any other woman that had ever been in his life, and she clearly felt the same way about him. Why in the world they couldn't work things out was beyond me, but I wasn't going to interfere. I knew if Pat heard me say that, he'd throw back his head and laugh, because he'd always thought that I was a bit of a Nosy Rosy, but he had no idea just how much I wanted to intervene in his love life.

As I drove back to the cabin, I wondered about the list that we'd just compiled. I had to admire my brother's ability to get information out of our suspects. I was afraid that my contributions were light compared to his, and he'd even taken on one of my suspects for me! I was going to have to step up my game if I wasn't going to let him leave me behind in the dust. I knew that it wasn't really a competition, but there were times as a twin that *everything* was a battle.

Traffic was fairly light, though I noticed that someone was behind me the entire time I drove back to my place. Was it just my imagination, though, or was someone really following me? I kept glancing back in my rearview mirror to see if I could make out the type of vehicle back there, but the car's headlights were indistinguishable from any other to me. If I were an automobile expert, I might have been able to tell from the distance between lights and their height off the ground, but alas, my abilities did not lie in that direction.

The truth would be known soon enough, anyway. If someone were following Pat home, they'd have an easy time blending in with other traffic, but no one else lived along my extensive driveway once I left the road, so if anyone was trying to sneak up on me, they'd have a devil of a time doing it.

I pulled into my drive, headed up a hundred yards, and then I pulled my Subaru over in the only spot wide enough to accommodate it without risking plummeting over the side of the mountain. After shutting off my headlights, I kept watch in my rearview mirror, waiting for something to happen.

I sat there until I was just about ready to give up on the whole thing when headlights finally appeared on the main road. Whoever was driving was going at a pretty sedate pace now.

Had I lost them? If I had, it must mean that whoever it was wasn't familiar with where I lived.

Then again, maybe they knew perfectly well where I'd been heading and had held back long enough to allow me to get home so they could proceed without being noticed.

I still couldn't make out the vehicle as it paused at my driveway entrance, but I could tell two things about it: it was big, and it was darkly tinted. That described many of our suspects' modes of transportation, but I couldn't help feeling that whoever was back there had killed Chester, no matter how irrational it was to believe that, given the lack of actual facts.

And then the headlights started to turn into my drive! Had I hidden myself well enough where I currently sat? If whoever was back there was intent on harming me, I'd inadvertently given them the perfect setup. After all, how much effort would it take the big SUV to pin me against the mountain and then deal with me at the driver's leisure? I was seriously rethinking my original plan when the headlights illuminated the inside of my car.

Clearly, I'd only thought I was out of sight where I'd parked, but the high beams of the car behind me clearly showed me that I'd been wrong.

What should I do now? Should I stand my ground and hope for the best, give up the hope that I'd been unseen and speed to the cabin, where I had the means to defend myself, or should I abandon my car altogether and take off on foot? No one knew my land better than I did, and I fully realized that I could probably lose my own siblings in the woods that surrounded my cabin. Someone who hadn't explored every nook and cranny of my land as I had didn't have a prayer of finding me once I made up my mind to disappear.

The decision was made for me before I had to act. The lights suddenly swung away as the driver did a U-turn and headed back the way they'd come.

I suddenly felt that I had to follow whoever it was, but there wasn't room for me to turn around!

So I did the only thing that I could do.

I started the engine and jammed my car into reverse, hoping that I could stay on my drive until I got to the main road. As I drove the hundred yards backward, trying to balance my need for speed with the desire to get there in one piece, I fought the steering wheel as though it were alive in my hands. Nearing the road, I felt my front left tire start to slip over the edge, and I realized that I'd cut things a little too fine. Staring back toward where the cabin stood in the distance, I managed to overcorrect just as I came to the end of my driveway.

Before I could pull all the way into the road, a different pair of headlights lit up the inside of my car as though it were noon, and a horn nearly jarred my teeth out of my mouth as a massive beast rushed past.

I'd almost hit a tractor-trailer in my zeal to catch whoever had been following me!

I waved my apologies to the driver, though they were long gone by the time my hand went up, and I drove back up the road to my cabin, considerably more slowly this time.

My hands were shaking slightly the entire way, and I felt my legs go a little wobbly when I got out of my Subaru, but I managed to steady myself on the car and made my way toward the front door without further incident. The Christmas lights were a welcome sight as I walked up onto the porch alone.

It was good to be home again.

<hr />

I could have fixed myself a four-course meal, but there was no way that was going to happen tonight. I'd been known on occasion to make a real feast just for myself, even putting out the fine china I'd inherited from my folks, but tonight, it was going to be a bowl of cereal and sitting on the couch watching old episodes of ancient sitcoms on my computer. I thought about giving Pat a call to tell him what had happened, but I knew that he'd overreact, and besides, if there was any justice in the world at all, he wasn't going to be alone. I finally decided that I could wait until the morning to report what had happened, if I decided to tell him at all. The entire episode may have been born out of my paranoia, and I'd feel like a fool if I told Pat.

I couldn't stay focused on the TV shows though, and after sampling and abandoning three different books that I'd enjoyed reading in the past, I decided that I just didn't have the attention span for anything too trying tonight. Instead, I grabbed a blanket from the couch, turned off all the lights in the cabin, and headed outside. Nestled into my rocking chair on the front porch, I sat there in silence as I listened to the sounds of the woods all around me. As far as I was concerned, it was the most beautiful, haunting lullaby that anyone could ever ask for. What

Pat found alarming was reassuring to me, and I let the sounds and scents of my surroundings envelop me.

Without realizing what was happening, I drifted slowly off to sleep.

When I woke up an hour later, I realized that the day had been more exhausting than I'd realized. I went back inside, and in short order I was in my pajamas, tucked snuggly into my bed in my loft with the stars just overhead, framed in my skylight.

There would be plenty of time to deal with everything that had happened tomorrow.

Tonight, I needed to sleep, and I let it come gleefully, nodding off with the images of the dancing night sky fresh in my mind.

CHAPTER 15: PAT

"**W**OULD YOU LIKE SOME TEA?" I offered Molly after she took a seat on my sofa. "I've got three or four kinds, so I'd be more than happy to make whatever you'd like."

"No, thanks. You know what? Sure. Why not? I'll have whatever's handy." Her voice sounded nervous as she spoke, something that puzzled me. We'd dated off and on since junior high, and we must have been alone together a thousand times. Why would she be jumpy now? As I made the tea for us, I began to wonder about why Molly was really in my apartment above the Iron. Did she want to get back together? If she did, was that something I even wanted? It took only an instant of thought to know that of course I did. I was in love with her, no matter how difficult it was for us to keep things going in the long run. As far as I was concerned, there was nobody else for me, and I knew it. She'd taken a brave step in coming here, so did I really have to make her be the one to declare her love first? I took a deep breath and got ready to tell her how I felt when she beat me to the punch and spoke first.

"Pat, we've got to end this thing between us, whatever it is, once and for all, tonight. I'm not going to be able to move on until I get some closure. We've been a part of each other's lives for so long that I have a hard time imagining going on without you, but we both know that we're never going to be able to make it work."

"You came here to dump me, and we aren't even dating?" I asked incredulously.

"I'm sorry. I just can't keep going on like this." She stood and headed for the door.

I didn't know what to say. I was totally dumbfounded. I'd been about to declare my feelings for her, and she dumped me before I had the chance to say one word. "What about your tea?" I asked her. *Are you serious?* I asked myself. *She tells you that she's done with you forever, and you ask her about a hot beverage? Have you completely lost your mind?*

"No, thanks. If you don't mind, I'll show myself out. Good-bye, Pat."

"Bye," I said. I felt as though I were in the middle of a nightmare, and I kept hoping that any second I'd wake up.

Unfortunately, the conversation had been real enough.

I didn't know what to do, so I did the only thing that made any sense to me at all.

I called my twin sister.

⊷⊖◇⊝⊶

"Hello?" she asked in more of a question than a statement.

"I woke you up, didn't I?"

"Of course not," she said, doing her best to hide the fact that she'd been asleep when I called.

"Go back to bed, Annie. This will wait until tomorrow."

"What is it, Pat? I'll never be able to get back to sleep if you don't tell me what happened this instant."

"Molly just dumped me," I said, blurting out the words.

"What? I didn't even realize that you two had gotten back together."

"That's the thing. We didn't."

"Patrick, you are making no sense whatsoever. Take a deep breath and tell me what happened."

"After you left, we came upstairs to my apartment. I suddenly realized just how much Molly meant to me and that I needed her in my life again. I was about to tell her that when she told me that she was finished with me, once and for all."

"What did you say when she said that? Did you at least try to change her mind?"

"Actually, I asked her if she'd like some tea," I admitted.

"What? Why on earth did you do that?"

"Annie, I was working on autopilot at that point. I'd started making tea, and it was all that I could think to do. She must have thought that I was an utter idiot." I could feel the emotion creeping into my voice as fresh tears trickled down my cheeks. I hadn't even realized that my ex-girlfriend still had that kind of power over me, and now that I did, it was too late to do anything about it. "Sis, you've got to help me. What am I going to do?"

"Do you want my honest advice, or do you want to hear platitudes and comforting talk that might help you sleep better tonight?" she asked me.

"I want the truth, no matter how brutal it might be," I said. I knew that I could count on Annie to deliver just that, even if it was another body blow after what I'd just gone through.

"Don't accept it," she said simply and without embellishment.

"What? How can I do that? She was pretty clear that she was done with me, once and for all."

"I heard what you said, but Pat, you need to respectfully tell her that you aren't ready to give up. Then you need to explain to her exactly how you feel about her and that you want her back in your life, whatever it takes." Annie had sincerely promised not to meddle in my love life years ago, but I'd asked for her opinion this time, and she hadn't held anything back.

"Let me ask you something. How long have you known that I was still in love with her?" I asked my sister.

"Since the moment you first saw her back in junior high school."

"That was a long time ago," I said softly.

"That doesn't mean that anything's changed," she said.

"When should I do it? How do I even approach her? Should I bring her flowers and balloons, or is that too corny? I have to do it face to face, don't I? Of course I do. Man, it's going to hurt when I do it, because I have a hunch that it is not going to go well for me at all. Any advice you have for me would be greatly appreciated."

"Sorry, but I've said all that I can say on the matter. The rest is up to you," Annie answered.

"What? You've been dying to give me advice about my life for years, and now that I'm telling you I need it, you're holding back on me?"

"Patrick, I love you like a brother—"

"I am your brother, you nit," I told her. It was a classic joke between us that never got old, but I found very little humor in anything at the moment.

"Don't interrupt me. Like I said, you mean the world to me, but you've got to do this by yourself. If it doesn't come from your heart, then it's not going to work."

"Do you honestly think that if I'm sincere enough, Molly will give me another chance?"

The pause was long enough to make me wonder if we'd lost our connection. When Annie finally spoke, her voice was full of sadness. "I don't know." The words were spoken like an execution, and I felt my heart die a little as I took them in.

"But I still have to at least try, don't I?" I asked softly.

"No matter what the final outcome is, you can't let it end like this," Annie said, and I knew that she was right.

"Thanks. I know just what to do. Go back to sleep."

"Aren't you going to at least run your plan by me first?" Annie asked.

"No time. I'll tell you what happened in the morning."

"As if I'll have any chance of getting back to sleep tonight," she protested.

I didn't even reply. I hung up the phone, grabbed my truck keys, and headed out of the Iron. I knew if I put off what I had to do for one second longer than was absolutely necessary, I'd lose my nerve—and any chance I ever had of getting back with Molly.

It was time to see her, and I meant right now.

———— ◆◇◆ ————

When Molly answered her door, I could see that she'd been crying. In a way, it made me feel a little better. After all, she hadn't been able to cast me away without consequence, pain, or remorse, so at least that was something. She looked genuinely surprised to see me. "Pat, what are you doing here?"

"We can't end things like this, Molly. I love you. I always have, and I always will. I need you in my life. Give me just one more chance. We can make it work. I know we can."

She was about to answer when I heard a man's voice coming from her living room. "Molly? Are you okay? Who is it?"

She closed the door a bit, just poking her head through the opening. "I'm sorry, Pat."

"Yeah, I can see that." I knew that I'd been beaten, and what was worse, that I'd even already been replaced. "I won't keep you. It was important that I at least tried. Have a good life. I hope whoever is in there treats you as well as you deserve. I guess this really is good-bye."

I turned and started to walk away, and I nearly made it back to my truck before I looked back at her.

She was already gone, and the door was closed.

I wasn't a big fan of metaphors, but I'd just been hit over the head with one.

More doors had been shut than the one in front of me, and

the sad truth was that there was nothing I could do about any of them.

I'd waited too long to tell Molly how I felt about her, and now it was too late.

She'd wanted to move on, and clearly, that's exactly what she was doing.

I was going to have to find some way to get over her as well, whether I liked it or not.

I didn't have the heart to call Annie back.

I'd deal with it tomorrow.

For now, all I wanted to do was go home and lose myself in self-pity and despair.

I figured that I at least had that coming to me.

CHAPTER 16: ANNIE

WHEN I GOT TO THE Iron the next morning well before I usually arrived, I was surprised to find my brother already sweeping the hardwood floor inside. We'd rescued the wood from an old factory building two towns over, and it gave the Iron that look of ancient authenticity that we'd been striving for. I loved the way the floors looked, though Pat had actually suggested that we refinish them after we'd had them laid at our place. I talked him out of it, and he'd come to thank me for stopping him from doing something atrocious, sanding away the decades of patina that had taken so much effort to build up.

"You're getting an early start on things this morning," I said as I took off my light jacket and hung it on the rack back by my workstation.

"I couldn't sleep," he said, refusing to make eye contact.

I could see that he was in pain, and I didn't need any special twin powers to catch it. I put a hand on his broom, effectively stopping him in his tracks. "What happened last night?"

"I don't want to talk about it," he said as he struggled to pull the broom out of my hand. I wasn't about to give in that easily, though.

"Did you at least try to talk to her again after we hung up?" I asked him. "You could have called her, Pat."

"I did more than that. I went to see her to declare my undying love."

"What did she say when you did that?" I was proud of my

brother for taking such a big step, and I knew how hard it must have been on him.

"That's the thing, Annie," he said, his heart breaking with every word. "Someone else was already there at her place with her by the time I got there. I was too late. I've lost her forever."

I dropped the broom and hugged my brother tightly. I knew, more than anyone, how much Molly meant to him, and I could hear in his voice that he indeed thought that he'd lost his last opportunity to be with her.

"Forever is an awfully long time, Pat," I said softly.

"I finally realized that I can't spend the rest of my life waiting for her," he answered. "She made it clear how she felt. Even if she breaks up with this guy, the two of us are never getting back together."

There was nothing to say to that, so I remained silent, still holding him, doing my best to offer whatever comfort I could. "Are you going to be okay?"

"I don't know," Pat said as he pulled away and discreetly wiped a few tears from his cheeks. "But I'll have to figure out a way to be, won't I? Thanks. You helped a lot."

"I don't see how," I replied in all honesty.

He laughed at my comment, a sound that lightened my own heart. "You being here and having my back is more valuable to me than all the gold in the world."

"You'd do the same thing for me," I said, knowing that even if the whole world turned against me, I'd always have my twin by my side. Pat was right; having someone nearby who loved and supported him was the most comforting thing in the world, and I felt bad about all those untold millions and millions of people who didn't have the luxury of having a twin of their very own.

By the time Edith and Skip came in for work, we had the place ready to greet our customers for the day. Both of our employees wanted to chat about the murder, but neither my brother nor I were in any mood to talk. They quickly got the hint, even Skip, and as they went about prepping their own work for the day, they made sure to keep the conversation light as they both avoided discussing what had happened to Chester Davis just a few feet away from where we were all working.

———◦✕◦———

"Throw an extra order of bacon on the griddle for me," Les Hodges ordered as he mulled over his breakfast choices. "I feel like splurging today."

"Any reason in particular?" I asked him as I retrieved three extra slices from the small built-in fridge by the range. I had a larger refrigerator/freezer in back, but I liked having that meal's supplies close at hand.

"It's a beautiful morning. Isn't that reason enough?" Les asked.

I glanced outside and saw that the rain was coming down in buckets. If this kept up, we'd all be drowning soon. "Liquid sunshine, is that it?"

"Annie, I run a landscaping service," Les said. "The more rain we get, the more grass we cut and the more money I make. Things have been kind of dry lately, so I say bring on the rain."

"Speak for yourself," Thad Jennings said three stools over. "It's not good for everyone."

"What's the matter, are your footings underwater again?" Les asked him.

"No, we got them poured two days ago, but my masons were supposed to start on the basement today, so it's quite literally going to be a wash."

"Hey, you're the one who decided to build houses for a living, not me," Les said.

"Shut up, Lester," Thad said, though the words were delivered with a good-natured smile.

That ended that conversation when Lester wouldn't answer.

I went back to the griddle, monitoring pancakes, hash browns, and bacon, while I had biscuits in the oven and eggs cooking in two different skillets on the burners. Coffee was percolating away, and I was happy to be in my element. I liked things when they were busy; it was more of a challenge to my talents and skills as a short-order cook when the Iron was hopping.

I was plating up Thad's order and getting ready to pivot it and make the delivery when someone caught my eye coming into the Iron. What was Bryson Oak doing here? I thought he was going to stop and chat with my brother, but instead, he headed straight for the lone empty stool at my counter without even breaking his stride.

"Should I come around and get that myself?" Thad asked gently, reminding him that I hadn't delivered his food yet.

I hadn't even realized that I'd stopped mid-delivery. "Sorry about that. I must have zoned out for a second."

"Don't worry about it. It happens to everyone," Thad said reassuringly.

"Remind me never to buy one of your houses," Les said.

"No worries there. You couldn't afford one," Thad shot back.

"I've got more money than you think."

"I know, everything's green in your line of work," Thad said, and then he started in on his breakfast. Les must have known better than to engage him while he was eating. Besides, he didn't have any reason to reply when I put his meal down in front of him soon after, extra bacon included. Both men were too busy eating to jaw at each other, which was fine with me.

"Hey, Bryson," I said as one of our suspects slid onto the stool. "What can I get you?"

"How about coffee to start?" he suggested.

"You have to order food or give up your seat," Les said to him as he pointed his fork in Bryson's direction. "That's the rule around here."

"Nobody's waiting, Les," I said. I was in no hurry to have Bryson leave, and I was willing to break one of my own rules to make sure that it didn't happen.

Bryson shook his head. "No, he's right. How about a gravy biscuit and two scrambled eggs?"

"Coming right up," I said. It was an easy order to prepare, and as soon as I delivered it, I was going to do a little different kind of grilling.

I didn't have to, though.

Les did it for me.

"That was a lucky break for you, what happened to Chester," Les said as he stared hard at Bryson. Les and Chester had been good friends, so his cutting remark didn't surprise me, nor did it catch Bryson off guard.

"I didn't particularly like him, that's true enough, but I didn't kill the man," Bryson said icily as he met Lester's gaze.

"Come on, Bryson, it went deeper than that, and there's no use trying to hide it. He beat you out of one too many land deals, and to beat all that, you started dating his ex-wife. That's about as nasty a rivalry as it gets, if you ask me."

"Nobody did, though, did they?" He sat there for a few seconds without another word until he suddenly spoke again. "Julia didn't have anything to do with my competition with Chester. Business was business. You're also forgetting that I beat Chester plenty of times myself. He may have won the last one, but I had my share of victories, too."

"The business stuff I'll buy," Thad said, putting in his own two cents. "But dating the man's ex just to get back at him is dirty dealing in anyone's book."

"Have you idiots seen Julia Crane?" Bryson asked. "She's beautiful, smart, and funny. Chester was a fool to let her go, but I wasn't complaining. His loss was my gain."

"So he did have something to do with you dating her," Les said. The two men, bantering with each other earlier, had now united in going after Bryson.

"He introduced us," Bryson said, his face beginning to redden. "Did you two hens come here to cluck or to eat?" His voice was growing louder with each syllable, and I could see hints of his temper rising to the surface. This was a lot more interesting than what I would have been able to get out of him.

Bryson's raised voice lifted a few eyebrows, and not just from his two combatants. He must have realized how he was beginning to look to everyone else, because his next words were spoken in a much calmer fashion. "Guys, I understand you're feeling pain from the loss of your friend, but I didn't do it."

In a soft voice that I nearly missed, Les said, "So you say."

Was Bryson going to react, or was he going to let it go?

I glanced back and saw that he was mulling it over, and then his shoulders slumped a little. Apparently he was going to let it go.

Too bad. I would have loved to see him in his full rage, because that's what it would have taken to hit Chester in the back of the head with my favorite frying pan, as far as I was concerned.

I plated Bryson's meal and delivered it, along with the check.

He nodded his thanks, and then he dug in, clearly happy to have an excuse not to carry on those particular conversations.

Now was the opportunity to ask him the last question that my brother hadn't been able to get an answer for.

"Sorry about the guys," I told Bryson as sympathetically as I could manage. "It's understandable that everyone's talking about what happened to Chester, especially around here."

"I get it," Bryson said between bites, "but it's got nothing to do with me."

"Maybe it does, maybe it doesn't," Les said.

Bryson chose to ignore him again, which I thought was a pretty sound policy.

"We've all been sharing when we saw him last," I said. "I myself spoke to him here at the store the day before yesterday. How about you?" I stood there like a statue, not caring if anything on the griddle was burning. I wanted an answer, and I wasn't moving until I got one.

"I already told your brother that I saw him that day myself," Bryson admitted.

"Really? What did you two chat about?" I asked before Les or Thad could chime in. Since neither one of them was on my list of suspects, I didn't care what either man had to add to the conversation. The details Bryson had given my brother about his last conversation with the murder victim had been pretty limited, so I wanted to follow up to see if I could get anything more out of him.

"I ran into him out in your parking lot, as a matter of fact," Bryson finally admitted.

"What did you talk about? Did you discuss the land deal he beat you out on?"

"As a matter of fact, business didn't occupy our entire conversation. It was mostly about Julia."

This was starting to get interesting, to more folks than just me. Everyone eating at the bar suddenly got quiet as we waited to hear Bryson's answer. "That's not what you told my brother. What did he say about her?" I asked him.

"Can you blame me? Julia was standing right there. Anyway,

Chester told me to back off, that she was too good for me, and that I'd better do as he said, or I'd regret it."

"Are you saying that the murder victim threatened you the day before he was killed?" I asked him.

Clearly Bryson hadn't thought things through that far. He'd been trying to make himself into the victim in our eyes, but he'd failed at it rather spectacularly. "That's not what I meant."

"That's sure what it sounded like to me," Les chimed in. "What did you do, decide to take him out before he could come after you? Why'd you have to hit him from behind, Bryson? Surely he at least deserved to see it coming."

"I can see here that I'm doomed no matter what I say," Bryson said angrily. "You people have already tried and sentenced me for Chester's murder, so what good are my protests going to do me?" He pulled a twenty out of his wallet and threw it on the counter, though his meal was only partially eaten.

"You need to pay Pat up front," I said.

"For what I'm leaving, you can do it yourself," Bryson said, and then he stormed out the back, not even bothering to go through the front, where my brother was waiting for him.

"What was that all about?" Pat asked as he hurried toward me.

"Bryson had to go all of a sudden," I said as I handed my brother the bill and the twenty. "Here you go."

He glanced at the amount I'd written in. "This is way too much."

"Put what's left in the jar for the animal shelter," I said as I started to clean the plates away from Bryson's spot. It had been an interesting conversation in more ways than one, and I wondered if any of our other suspects would happen by the Iron before we closed up for the day. It helped that just about everyone in town had to come by, to check their mail if nothing else.

And if they came in, either Pat or I would make them pay

with an answer to at least one of our questions before we'd let them get away.

———— ❦ ————

We were finished with our breakfast rush, and the early lunch crowd was just starting to make its way into the Iron. I always served breakfast whenever I was open, but I wouldn't serve my lunch specials before 10:45 a.m. My regulars knew that, and they would never try to order early, but sometimes I had to educate newcomers. Any order would be valid now though, since it was five minutes before eleven. I'd checked on my Dutch ovens a little earlier, and the food was finished and simmering away nicely, ready and waiting. That was one of the great things about cast iron; I'd been able to turn the ovens off, and the heat retained by the iron was enough to keep things nice and toasty as diners began to order their meals.

"Is this seat taken?" someone asked as my back was turned to the bar facing the grill.

"If it's empty, it's yours," I said, and then I turned to see who was talking. It was the attorney Pat and I had met earlier. I knew he had a long fancy name, but Rob was all that I could remember without digging out his business card. "Welcome back. Is this business or pleasure?"

"Mostly pleasure at the moment. Chester's spoken so highly of your food that I had to give it a try for myself while I was in town. What's on the lunch menu today?"

"We have our standard offerings of hamburgers, hot dogs, and grilled cheese. The special is roasted chicken, potatoes, carrots, and onions, all made in a cast iron Dutch oven."

"What would you recommend?" he asked.

"Everything's good," I answered with a grin, "but in my mind, you can't beat the chicken. I use a spice mix I get from a guy up in New York State, and it's outstanding."

"Then that's what I'll have, and some sweet tea as well. I assume that it's on the menu, too, am I right?"

"Would we be in the South if it weren't?" I asked as I poured a glass for him. He took a long sip and then let out a satisfied acknowledgment.

"Perfect. It's just the way I like it," he said.

I pulled one of my Dutch ovens out of the left oven and dished him out a nice portion of chicken and vegetables. Of all the things I prepared for lunch, this meal was one of my favorites.

As I put the plate in front of him, he took in the aromas and smiled broadly. "It smells like paradise."

"If you think it smells good, wait until you taste it," I answered.

I had other orders, but I wanted to see how he reacted to his first bite. From the look of sheer pleasure on his face, I assumed that it was a hit.

We chatted a little as I served my other customers, and when he was finished, I offered, "I've got some banana pudding for dessert, and some cherry tart cake that was made fresh in cast iron yesterday."

"Why the fascination with cast iron?" he asked me. "Not that I'm complaining. That was unbelievably good."

"Pat and I started collecting it when we were young, and we were both cooking on campfires before we could drive. There's something about iron that makes just about everything better. If I have a choice, I use cast iron over any other cookware."

"Aren't you afraid of getting too much iron in your diet?" he asked after taking a sip of tea.

"My doctor knows how I eat, and he laughs whenever I have blood work done. My iron is slightly elevated, but it's still better than loading up on vitamins I don't need through pills and supplements."

"I have to admit that I really like the delivery system," Rob said. He looked around and saw that the crowd at my bar was tapering off. "Annie, do you have a minute to spare to talk to me?"

"That, and not much more. Is it about Chester?" I wasn't eager to talk about my late friend in front of anyone else, but stepping away from the range was problematic.

"Actually, this is for me. I'm looking for a nice piece of land I can build a cabin to escape on, and I was wondering if you could help. I heard that you lived in one yourself, so I figured you might be able to point me in the right direction."

"Where did you hear that?" I asked him. Had the attorney been asking around about me? Did that have something to do with Chester, or did he have other, more personal reasons in mind?

"Sorry, I didn't realize that it was a secret," he said with a smile.

"It's not. It's just that small towns have folks who like to talk." I had to stop being so paranoid. "Forgive me for saying so, but you don't look like the outdoorsy type."

"Don't let the suit fool you," he said. "My uncle had a cabin in the woods where I'm from in West Virginia, and some of my happiest summers were spent there. I've been looking for a good place to build one of my own, and this area is just about perfect for what I want."

"You said that you wanted it as an escape, so is it going to be a full-time residence or just a place to get away to on weekends?"

He shrugged. "To start with, I'm keeping my job, but eventually I hope to move there full time."

"Are you looking for anything in particular on the land? Streams will cost you more, and lake frontage even more than that."

Rob shook his head. "I just want to be surrounded by trees in the mountains. I don't need much more than five or ten acres, but I'd like to feel as though I'm out in the wilderness alone. I have more than my share of cell phones, television, and traffic in my daily life, so I'd love a place to get away."

Here was a man after my own heart. "I might be able to help. Let me make a few calls, and I'll get back to you."

There was something else on his mind—I could see it in his eyes. Was he going to ask me out? "Is there anything else I can do for you?" I asked him as I cleared away his plate and left him his bill.

"I know it's asking a lot, but is there any way I could see the cabin where you live? It might help me plan my own place."

"Isn't that putting the cart before the horse?" I asked him. "After all, you don't even have any land yet."

Was that disappointment flickering across his gaze? "Sorry. You're right."

I felt bad about refusing him. "Maybe it would help you after all. Can you come out tonight around eight? I have some things to do after work, but I should be free by then."

His smile reminded me of a little boy's grin. "That would be great."

I wrote the directions down on a napkin and handed it to him. "I'll see you then."

"Thanks. I can't tell you how much I appreciate this."

"It's my pleasure."

As he walked up front to pay his bill, I couldn't help but watch him. I thought our conversation had been private until Cora Yount looked up from her book four stools down and spoke up. "He's a live one, Annie. It looks like you've got yourself a date, young lady."

I shook my head, but I couldn't hide the hint of a grin. "You read too many romance novels, Cora."

She grinned at me. "That's impossible. There's no such thing as too many. You want some pointers from a worldly old gal willing to share?"

I laughed out loud. "Thanks, but I'm sure that I'll be fine on my own."

"Suit yourself, but trust me, it's your loss," she said with a smile, and then she turned back to her book.

I found myself getting excited about the prospect of showing the attorney around my land and my cabin, but I knew that I might be reading too much into the situation. Maybe he was just coming out to see my setup and nothing else.

Then again, a girl could always hope, couldn't she?

It had been too long since I'd had any romance in my life.

Maybe the attorney was exactly what I needed.

CHAPTER 17: PAT

D ESPITE WHAT HAD HAPPENED THE day before, things were
slowly beginning to get back to normal at the Iron. Annie
was at the grill, Edith was at her post wrapping up the day's
business at the post office, and Skip was scanning the shelves of
my part of the place searching for something to restock. One
of our customers had once called us Maple Crest's very own
mini-superstore, but I didn't take offense. After all, the town,
probably even the county, was just too small to support one of
those huge twenty-four-hour-a-day operations, which suited me
just fine. Annie and I had found the perfect niche in a place
populated enough to need us but not large enough for someone
else to try to come in and take away our customer base. I was
starting to feel pretty good about our situation again, which was
a sign that something bad was about to happen.

And sure enough, not five minutes later, it did.

———— ✦❖✦ ————

"Patrick, we need to talk," my sister Kathleen said when she
came into the Iron that afternoon.

"In what capacity?" I asked her, since she was still in uniform.

"My official one, unfortunately," she answered tersely. "I
believe that you and I are about to have ourselves a problem."

It was never good when my older sister started talking like a
character from an old-fashioned crime novel, so I braced myself

for the onslaught. Her use of my full first name was never a good sign, either.

"I can't imagine why that might be," I said, trying to keep it as casual as I could, given what Annie and I had been up to. I'd been afraid of something like this happening from the very beginning, and it appeared that it had taken Kathleen less time than I'd anticipated to get wind of what my twin and I were up to.

"Oh, I bet if you take a second and think about it real hard, you'll know what I'm talking about."

Was she waiting for me to confess before she actually confronted me? Surely she knew me better than that. It hadn't worked when we'd been kids, and it wasn't about to succeed now. If she wanted to wait me out, she was in for a long afternoon.

"Sorry, but I don't have any idea what you're talking about," I said as I started straightening up the counter where the register sat among a dozen impulse-purchase items ready to be grabbed up by our customer base on their way out the door. It was amazing how much extra income that one little trick generated over the course of a month.

"Patrick Marsh, you may think this is funny, but you need to realize here and now that I'm dead serious."

I looked into her gaze and saw that there was no room for messing around. She was genuinely upset with Annie and me, and if I could fix it, I had to, even if it meant raising her blood pressure a few more points by confessing what my twin and I had been up to. It was, in many ways, the three of us against the world. We'd always been close, but after our folks had died, the bond we'd formed was nearly unbreakable, no matter how hard Annie and I might have pushed it at times.

"I understand," I answered. "Give me one second." I turned to Skip. "Hey, I need you up here for a minute."

He gladly dropped what he was doing and joined me. "What's up, chief?"

"How many times do I have to tell you that I'm not your chief?" I asked him with a grin. "I'm your boss, and hopefully your friend, but I'm not your chief."

"Sorry. I guess you'll have to tell me a few more times," Skip answered with a smile of his own.

"Take over the front for a minute. I need to speak with my sister."

"Sure thing. Should I get Annie for you?" he asked.

"Not that sister. That one," I said as I pointed to Kathleen, who was standing several steps away from the front counter, waiting impatiently for me.

"Okay. Whatever you say, ch...boss...Pat." He clearly couldn't make up his mind what he wanted to call me.

"Do you mind if we step outside?" I asked Kathleen as I approached her, and then, without waiting for her to reply, I said, "Trust me, it'll be easier to have this conversation if we don't have an audience." The real reason I'd asked her to move our talk outside was because I didn't want Annie joining us, at least not yet. My twin had a tendency to lead with her mouth sometimes, and Kathleen wasn't that much better. I'd always been the peacemaker growing up, and I didn't see any reason for that to change now.

"Fine," she said impatiently. "We can do it wherever you want to, but we're going to have this conversation."

I led her out the front door, and then we both neatly sidestepped the spot where Chester had been murdered just a few days before. I started playing with ideas about how to break the news to Kathleen that Annie and I were digging into Chester's murder when she did it for me.

"What were you two thinking, Pat?" Kathleen asked, lighting into me before I even had the chance to come up with some kind of defense. "Murder is serious business. I expect something like this out of Annie, but I always thought that you were the rational one of the pair. You don't have any business digging into Chester's death. That's my job, and you should leave it to the professionals."

She was expecting me to try to mollify her from the beginning, and I even started to do just that when I suddenly stopped in mid-thought. "Kathleen, Chester was murdered right there," I said as I pointed to the spot. No matter how much I'd scrubbed the area earlier, I had a hunch that it would never be clean enough for me again. "Whoever did it used Annie's pot for a reason. The killer had to have known that one of us would find Chester's body. I wish that it had been me and not our sister, but either way, we're both in the middle of this whether we want to be or not."

Kathleen's scowl began to ease. "Is she really taking it that hard? She looks fine to me."

"Everything is not as it seems," I said. "Whoever chose this spot did it intentionally. Can there be any doubt in your mind that the killer is the one who dragged us into this? What makes you think that this wasn't a warning that one of us would be next? When I heard Annie's cries out here yesterday morning, I rushed out to find her pinned to the floor by a dead man." My older sister started to say something, but I held my hand up in the air for her silence. To my surprise, she quieted down instantly so I could finish my thought. "I had to pull Chester off of her. I don't know how many dead bodies you've touched in your life, but that was a first for me, and I hope like anything that it's the last one as well."

"I understand that it was traumatic for both of you, but that's still no reason to go out on your own and start questioning my suspects."

I was keeping the fact that Chester had written us and

made the request out of the conversation for the moment, but I planned on bringing it up sooner or later. "Out of curiosity, who was it that complained about us to you?"

"That's not really relevant," Kathleen answered curtly.

"Maybe not to you, but it matters to us."

"Pat, are you really going to speak for Annie as well?"

"About this, I'm fairly confident that we're in full agreement," I told her. I kept looking at Kathleen expectantly, hoping that she'd crack and confess the name to me, but she was at least as good at playing things close to the vest as I was.

"Who exactly have you spoken with so far?" Kathleen asked.

I shrugged. "I admit that we've had a few innocent conversations, but it's not like we lined people up and started grilling them."

"That's not the way I heard it," Kathleen replied. "By the time I got inside Lydia's place, between the two of you, you'd already spoken to everyone I wanted to interview."

"Is that why you're so upset, because we beat you to the punch?" As soon as I asked the question, I knew that I'd stepped over the line. I tried my best to withdraw the question, but it was too late.

"No, you prized idiot, I'm angry because you're interfering with me doing my job!" That statement was loud enough to rattle the windows a little, and I wondered if anyone had heard it inside the Iron.

"Take it easy, Sis," I said.

"Sheriff," Kathleen corrected me.

"Okay, Sheriff. When you speak with folks about Chester's murder, they see your uniform and all that stands for. When it's Annie or me talking to them, they're having a conversation with a friend, a neighbor, someone they don't readily associate with law enforcement. Are you telling me that we could each ask them the same questions and we'd get identical answers?"

"Of course not," she admitted, much to her credit. "That still doesn't mean that you have any right to interfere with what I'm doing."

"Frankly, I don't see how it could," I answered.

"Pat, are you being intentionally dense right now, or are you just yanking my chain?"

"Neither one," I said quickly. "I'm just trying to help you see how this could be a good thing, for you and for the investigation."

Kathleen's smirk was one that I was well familiar with. "This I've got to hear."

"There are a few ways that you can look at it if you take a step back from the situation. One, the questions we ask have no impact on your investigation, so basically no harm, no foul. Two, we get answers that you couldn't, and you learn more about the murder case with our assistance than you would have without it."

"How about the third possibility?" she asked me.

"What's that?"

"You ask questions, they get suspicious, and then they all clam up before I even get the first query out of my mouth."

"What happened, Sheriff? Did someone refuse to speak with you?"

"Of course not," she snapped. "That doesn't mean that I got anyone's full cooperation, though, and I attribute that directly to the fact that you and Annie were sniffing around my suspects before I had a chance to interview them for myself."

I could sympathize with her for feeling that way, but I didn't buy that it was a possibility. "Do you honestly think that the only reason anyone stonewalled you was because they'd already spilled their guts to Annie or me? Take my word for it. It didn't happen. Would you like to know what we were able to find out?" I knew that Annie wouldn't be too pleased with me for admitting to our big sister what we'd been up to, but what else could I do? I just hoped that she understood why I'd done it.

"How can I listen to your results in good faith? I don't know anything about your interview methodology, and I can't even be sure that someone didn't feed you a lie to convince you of their innocence. This world is much more complicated than yours."

"What do you mean by that?"

"Don't you dare take offense at what I'm saying," Kathleen replied. "All I meant,was that running the Iron and overseeing a murder investigation are two entirely distinctive things, and they take completely different skill sets."

"I'm not so sure about that. In the end, it all boils down to people skills, don't you think? If there's anything that qualifies Annie and me to do what we're trying to do, it's the fact that we know these people like you can't. We've seen them in this store at their best and, more importantly, at their worst. We have insights into how the minds of the people of Maple Crest think that you can't have. Regardless of whether it's right or wrong, when they see you, they think law enforcement officer, and when they see Annie and me, they think friends."

"I have friends in this town, too," she protested, though I knew that her limited circle of acquaintances was a sore point with her.

"I'm not denying it, but you wear a uniform, and you know as well as I do that means folks act differently around you. Why won't you take our help for what it's worth? What could it possibly hurt? We'll be sure you get full credit if we solve this case instead of you, if that's what you're worried about."

She got up in my face, and her words were scalding when they reached me. "Is that what you think? Patrick, you're an even bigger idiot than I thought you were, and that's saying something. I couldn't give a flip in the wind who finds Chester's killer, and that's the truth. What I don't want, what I couldn't live with, is the idea that you two root around into something where your noses don't belong, and one of you gets hurt or even killed. How could I ever forgive myself if something happened to either one of you?"

It was a softer side than I was used to seeing of my older sister, and it touched me a great deal. "We're being careful, Sis. Honest."

"What makes you think that Chester wasn't being just as cautious?" she asked me softly.

"There's one big difference that I can think of right off the bat," I said. "Chester didn't have you watching his back." It was time to tell Kathleen about the letter Chester had written Annie and me before he'd been murdered; I didn't feel as though I had any choice. "Chester *asked* us to do this for him, Kathleen. How could we say no?"

My older sister looked shocked. "How exactly did he do that? What did he do, contact you through a Ouija board?"

"No, it was something much more concrete than that. He wrote us a letter. The man knew that someone was after him, and he pleaded with us to find his killer. You might be able to ignore something like that, but Annie and I can't. If you have to lock us up to keep us from digging into his murder, then so be it, but that's the only way you're going to get us to back off, no matter how much we both love you."

Kathleen was silent for a long time as she processed the things I'd just told her. After a full minute, she said, "I need to see that letter."

I wasn't sure what I was going to do, but I was saved from making a decision, at least for that moment, when Annie walked out the door, her grill station abandoned so she could see what was keeping her brother and sister outside so long.

I knew that the ride was about to get considerably more bumpy.

CHAPTER 18: ANNIE

"**W**HAT'S THE BIG DISCUSSION OUT here about?" I asked as I saw my brother and older sister facing off on the front porch of the Iron. I turned to Pat and asked him, "Did you break down and tell her about what happened last night?"

"No, he didn't." Turning away from me to face our brother, Kathleen asked him, "Pat, what happened last night?"

"It was nothing," Pat said, trying to get me to shut up about what had happened with Molly. Like that was going to happen.

"Molly dumped him," I said simply.

"I didn't know they were even going out," Kathleen said.

"They weren't. That's probably why it stung so much," I replied.

"Molly is not the topic of our conversation," my brother said with real conviction. "Chester Davis is."

"Chester? What about him?" I asked, wondering what my brother had told our older sister about what we'd been up to lately.

"Drop the act, Annie," Kathleen said. "Pat spilled it all. I know everything."

"Everything?" I asked as I looked at Pat intently. Sometimes my twin had a problem saying no to our big sister, a problem that I'd never encountered myself.

"She knows we've been asking questions and why, but she doesn't have any of the details yet," Pat explained. "I'm sorry, but I couldn't keep her in the dark about it. I told her about the letter, too."

"Fine," I said, trying to come to grips with the fact that the sheriff, who also happened to be our sister, knew that we were digging into a murder case that we had no right to investigate. "I get it." I wasn't all that happy about the change in circumstances, but I'd known from the beginning that this moment was inevitable.

I just wasn't all that crazy about it happening now, particularly while the Iron was still open for business.

"Pat was just about to give me the letter you got from Chester," Kathleen said to me, and then she turned to our brother. "Where is it, Pat?"

"I've got it," I lied. I knew that Pat's copy was inside, but I wasn't about to get into this with Kathleen just yet. Had he even told her that there were two copies of it?

"Listen, I don't care who has it, I just want to see it for myself."

"Okay. We'll hand it over in one hour and twenty-seven minutes," I said after I looked at my watch.

"Think again, Annie. You'll give it to me right now," Kathleen insisted.

"Not without some background information first," I said. "You need to hear what we've done before you read it. Otherwise, you're going to dismiss everything we have to offer."

"I could always just lock you both up and *make* you give me the letter," she told me, and then she stared hard at Pat. Kathleen was no idiot; she knew that if one of us was going to break, it would be our brother. She didn't know him as well as I did, though. I couldn't imagine him going against what I'd just told her unless someone else's life was at stake.

"Pat, you need to do the right thing," the sheriff said.

He looked at me, and then he shrugged at her. "Sorry, but Annie's right. We don't have time to get into it right now, and you need to hear what we have to say before you see the letter Chester wrote us. If you feel the need to lock us up, then go ahead, but I've got to warn you, if you do that, we're not going to invite you to Thanksgiving dinner."

"That's five months away," Kathleen said. "I'll worry about it when it happens."

"Well then, how about our big Labor Day picnic? You can't come to that, either, if you put us both in jail," I retorted.

Kathleen studied him closely for a moment before replying. "You two think you're cute, don't you?"

"We've been told that we're both reasonably attractive, yes," he answered with a grin. "Face it, Kathleen. The only way we're going to cooperate is if you give us a little something, too."

"Besides, Chester wrote that letter to us, not to you," I chimed in. "Technically, we don't even have to let you see it." I thought it was a perfectly valid point given the circumstances, but evidently my siblings agreed that it was not.

"There's no reason to get snippy about it, Annie," Pat said.

"She's threatening to throw us in jail, and you're calling me snippy?"

"I'm just saying," Pat said, "no matter what, she's still our big sister."

"Fine," Kathleen said out of frustration. "I'll give in this time, but the second you lock the front door and send everyone else home, the three of us are going to have ourselves a long talk."

"Looking forward to it," I said as I hurried back inside. I'd left my station unmanned, something I almost never did, and I knew that I needed to get back to it fast. I was still glad that I'd gone outside; it was hard to tell what Pat would have told Kathleen if I hadn't been there to stop him.

I was happy with where we'd left things, but that joy quickly dissipated when I saw who walked into the Iron and headed for my grill an hour later.

Lydia and Franklin were visiting, and from the expressions on their faces, it didn't appear to be a friendly call.

———— ·——⊂⟨⟩⊃——· ————

"We'll take two specials, whatever you're serving," Lydia said as they sat down at the nearly deserted line of stools twenty minutes before we were due to close for the day. We were having one of our usual lulls, so at least there weren't many other diners there to eavesdrop on our conversation.

"Today, it's chicken," I said.

"I don't know. I'm not that big a fan of chicken," Franklin said. "I think I'd rather have a cheeseburger instead."

"Must you make everything complicated?" Lydia asked her brother.

"I don't want the chicken, Lydia. Live with it," he snarled. I pitied Chester watching them bicker his entire life. It must have been a nightmare for the good-natured man growing up.

"Fine. You may as well make it two cheeseburgers, instead," Lydia said.

"Just because I'm getting a burger doesn't mean that you have to," Franklin snapped.

"I honestly don't care what I have," Lydia said, and then she looked at me. "No offense."

"Why should I take offense?" I asked as sweetly as I could muster. I'd mastered the art of being agreeable with disagreeable customers a long time ago. My lack of sincerity with the miniscule percentage of the population that didn't love what I offered seemed to generally go unnoticed by those I was conning, so I made a game of being as friendly as humanly possible to the rudest batch of people that I faced. If nothing else, it usually tended to throw them off their games, if they even noticed what I was doing. "Two cheeseburgers, coming right up." They hadn't mentioned any sides, and I declined to suggest them. Those might take more time, and I didn't want them in the Iron when my sister returned. She'd think that we'd enticed them there or something equally ridiculous.

Lydia seemed to dismiss me as she turned to her brother and said in idle speculation, "I can't believe Bryson and Julia."

"I know," Franklin said, glancing at me out of the corner of his eye to be sure that I was listening. Apparently they were putting on a show for me. I only wished that I had popcorn to make their performances more enjoyable. "Chester must have felt betrayed by both of them."

"Bryson only dated her to get under our brother's skin. He'd been beaten too many times in business. It must have killed him when Chester snatched up another new property right under his nose yet again. From what I hear, when he's drinking, he loses his mind, so I'm not sure why anyone's surprised by what he might have done."

"Julia's no prize, either," Franklin said as he switched the conversation to their former sister-in-law. Lydia was almost plausible in her behavior, but she'd clearly been the one who'd gotten all the acting talent in their family. Franklin had overpracticed his part so much that he might as well have been reading his lines off cue cards. "She told him that she still loved him, and he just laughed at her. She must have wanted to kill him with her bare hands on the spot. The woman's been on medication for years, but I'm not sure that it's helped her any."

I'd put their burgers on the grill top after they'd decided on their orders, and it was time to flip them both over. After I did just that, I took two slices of cheddar and laid them on top of the cooked portions so the cheese could melt as the burgers finished cooking. I thought the show might be over, but apparently I was wrong.

"You know who else hated Chester?" Lydia asked her brother.

"Who?"

"Harper Gentry," she said.

"I thought they were dating," Franklin said, trying—and failing miserably—to convey a sense of surprise as he spoke.

"Didn't I tell you? He broke up with her the night before he died," Lydia said. "He told me in confidence that the girl was positively unstable! Poor Chester. Who knew there would be so many reasons people would want to harm him?"

I kept ignoring them as I lightly brushed some butter on each bun half before placing them on the grill to toast a little before their burgers were ready to be served.

"It just goes to prove that nobody loves you like your family does," Franklin said. Honestly, his acting was getting worse by the minute.

Lydia reached out and patted her brother's arm. "At least we honestly cared about him."

"We can both take comfort in that fact," he said.

I wasn't sure how much more of this I could take before I burst out laughing, but thankfully, their cheeseburgers were finally ready. I slid the patties between their respective buns, plated them, and then pivoted and delivered them to the brother and sister. "There you go."

Franklin lifted the top bun as some of the melted cheese clung to it. "This thing doesn't have anything on it."

"You didn't ask for any condiments," I said with a smile as I presented him with the check.

"Just eat it," Lydia said tiredly.

"Fine," he replied, and then he reached for the catsup and slathered it all over my perfect burger. He might as well have been eating shoe leather for all that he'd be able to taste it after he was finished with it. I used Angus beef, the best I could find, but in this case, it was all for naught.

Lydia eschewed the catsup, though, and took a bite of exactly what I'd prepared for her. "Hey, that's really tasty," she said, as though she had the right to be amazed that my food wasn't entirely dreck.

"I don't know. It's just like every other burger I've ever had," her brother replied.

I grabbed another squeeze bottle filled with catsup and put it near his plate. "Maybe you just need more of this."

"No, it's fine," he said. The idiot hadn't even realized that I'd been making fun of him. Honestly, that took some of the joy out of it.

He wolfed his burger down in four bites, while his sister ate hers slowly and carefully. Franklin's frustration and impatience with her were apparent after he'd finished his meal. "Aren't you finished yet?"

"I like to taste my food," she said primly.

He sat there another three minutes, sighing every ten seconds as his sister continued to eat. Finally, she must have grown tired of his attention. Pushing away a plate with a third of her burger still on it, she smiled at me and said, "That was delightful. Thank you."

"Come back any time," I said with a smile and an invitation that I didn't mean. It was what I told every customer, no matter how their dining experience had been. If Lydia and Franklin wanted to feed me what I was almost certain was false information, then they were going to have to pay us for the privilege.

I'd seen Pat watching the brother-and-sister act the entire time they'd been in our store, and he nearly sprinted for the cash register in front to take their money when they approached. After they were gone, barely stopping at the tip jar to put a few pennies and nickels in spare change in, my twin hurried back to me.

"What was that all about?"

"They came by for a late lunch," I said as I added a shrug.

"That's garbage and you know it," my brother replied. "I

heard some of what they were saying, and it had nothing to do with our cuisine."

"If you already heard them, why are you asking me now?"

"I just got bits and pieces of it," Pat acknowledged. "Our pesky customers kept interrupting my attempts to eavesdrop." He added the last bit with a grin, something I quickly reciprocated.

"You didn't miss much. You're right, by the way. They didn't come by for the food. Franklin must have used an entire bottle of catsup on his burger. It's amazing he could taste anything but tomatoes, sugar, and salt at all."

"What did they talk about?" Pat pushed.

"It's all basically what we already knew, with a few embellishments," I said as I started to scrape the griddle section of my range with the stone I used to keep the surface slick and stick free.

"Like what?" Pat asked. There were only two customers left in the store, and they were both looking at postcards over in Edith's section, though she'd left the Iron two hours earlier. Skip was there helping them, though, so I could see why Pat wasn't all that concerned about abandoning the front.

"They tried to act as though they were having a casual conversation, but it was clear that the entire thing was intended for my ears. According to them, Bryson is a mean drunk, Julia takes medication because she's crazy, and Harper is unbalanced on her own. Man, that pair gives brothers and sisters a bad name."

"Nobody would ever compare us to them," Pat said, and I hoped that he was right. My brother and I might snip at each other on occasion, but no one could deny the bond we shared that went way beyond our time in the womb.

I was about to say something in response when his cell phone rang. He must have turned the ringer on recently, because we both kept them set on vibrate during regular business hours. Pat glanced at the number, and then he said as he started to walk up front, "Sorry, Annie, but I have to take this."

"Is it Molly?" I asked him.

"I wish, though I'm afraid that's never going to happen again," he answered. "It's Harper."

"I wonder what she wants."

"I don't know, but I have the feeling that I'm about to find out."

CHAPTER 19: PAT

I LEFT ANNIE INSIDE THE IRON while I stepped outside to take Harper's phone call on the front porch. It wasn't as though I was trying to hide my conversation from her; I just knew that if I took it in front of her, she'd be interjecting with a great deal of input that I didn't need. "Hey, Harper."

"Pat, I need to speak with you. It's important. It's about Chester."

"I'd be happy to talk. Why don't you come by the Iron? Annie and I are still here."

She choked up a little before she replied. "I hope you understand, but I can't come there, not after what happened to Chester."

"I get that. No worries. Annie and I can meet you just about anywhere," I said. I'd heard conflicting stories about Harper and her relationship with Chester, and I wanted to pin her down on what had really happened between them the night before he'd been murdered.

"Can't you come alone?" Harper asked, her voice now barely above a whisper.

"What's wrong? Do you have a problem with my sister?" I asked her. Everyone knew that Annie and I were a team in nearly everything that we did, so asking us to split up was counterintuitive to everything we presented to the world.

"To be honest with you, she asked me some questions at Lydia's that I wasn't all that comfortable answering. The truth is that I've never felt as at ease around women as I have men. Could you come alone?"

I hated the idea of excluding Annie, but what choice did I have? "If you insist, but you should know that whatever you tell me, I'll just end up repeating to her."

"Once we have our talk, I don't care who you tell. How soon can you meet me?"

I glanced at my watch. "We have five more minutes to keep the Iron open, and after that, we have a few things we need to do before we can leave. How does five o'clock sound to you?"

"I'd rather it were now, but I suppose I can wait that long."

I wasn't sure how I was going to get Annie to agree to let me go alone, but I'd have to come up with something, or we were going to take a chance of losing some valuable information. "Where would you like to meet up, at your place?"

"I'd rather it be a little less visible to the world. How about if we go to one of the benches around the lake? There's one in particular just where the woods meet the water that I've always been fond of, and it should be practically deserted at that time of day."

I knew the spot. It was the most secluded bench around the lake—in all of the park, as a matter of fact. After dark, it was known as a hangout where teens went to profess their undying love to each other, among other activities, but it should be fairly empty before nightfall. Parsons Lake Park was one of the nicest things our little town had to offer. "Sounds good. I'll be there at five."

"Thank you. I'll see you soon."

When I disconnected the call, Annie was standing at the door, listening in to my side of the conversation. I hadn't noticed her until I was putting my phone away.

"So, she wants to get you alone at the most romantic spot in Maple Crest, does she?" my sister asked me.

"I'm sure she doesn't have anything like that in mind," I said.

"You never know. What I want to know is why you agreed to meet her alone."

"What could I do? You made her uncomfortable with your questions at Lydia's, and she said she felt as though she could trust me more." I hadn't meant to couch the information so negatively, but if Annie took offense, she didn't say anything about it.

"I didn't even think that I'd pressed her all that hard," my sister said. "Either she's a truly delicate little flower, or she has another reason to get you alone."

"I don't know what it could be. Her request didn't make me particularly suspicious," I said.

"That's why you've got me," Annie answered. "I'm paranoid enough for the both of us."

"Do you honestly think she wants to do me harm? That doesn't make any sense." I knew that my twin could overreact at times, but this was crazy, even for her.

"Let's think about this rationally. She's one of our murder suspects, true?"

"True, but that doesn't necessarily mean—"

"Let me finish," Annie insisted. "Next, she knows that we're investigating Chester's murder."

"She probably has a clue," I agreed.

"Let me ask you something. If Franklin had approached you and asked you to meet him at an isolated spot alone, what would your reaction have been?"

"I'm not sure," I replied. "I suppose there's a chance that I wouldn't have agreed to it."

"You wouldn't go anywhere near that park if he'd been the one asking, and you know it," Annie said. "Just because Harper is a woman doesn't mean that you should take her innocence for granted, or turn your back on her, for that matter. I don't have to tell you what happened to Chester when he offered someone the back of his head, do I?"

I remembered that pool of blood by the cast iron pan, and I shuddered a little at the thought. "Don't worry, I'll be careful."

"You bet you will, because I'm going with you," Annie declared.

"If you come along, she's not going to say anything," I insisted.

"If I don't, there's a chance that something bad might happen to you, and I've gotten used to having you around, Pat, so I'm not ready to say good-bye just quite yet."

I thought about what she was saying, but Harper had presented it as an all-or-nothing scenario.

While I was still considering how to put my feelings into words, Annie followed up with, "If the roles were reversed, if she'd insisted on speaking with me, would you have agreed to let me go by myself?"

"That's different," I said.

"How, pray tell, is that?" I knew that look. Annie wasn't messing around. She really was concerned about my welfare, and she was willing to push me to ensure it.

"You're right. I know you're right. But I still have to go, and it has to be alone."

She looked long and hard at me, and then my twin sister nodded. "You're right."

"I'm sorry, I'm not sure that I heard you. What did you just say?"

"I said that you were right. Don't act so surprised. It was bound to happen sooner or later." Annie glanced at her phone. "Let's close so we can get started finishing up for the day before Kathleen comes back."

"Too late," I said as the sheriff drove up in her cruiser, ready to see Chester's letter.

"Where is it?" Kathleen asked a moment after she got out of her official police vehicle.

"Hi, Sis," Annie said cordially. "How are you doing?"

"Save the pleasantries. I'm here for that letter."

I looked around, and though I couldn't see anyone nearby, I knew that the killer could be hiding in the trees next to the store listening to everything we said. I was going to have to rethink using the front porch for privacy, and not just because of what had happened to Chester. "Can we at least take this inside first?"

"Okay, but I'm not in the mood for any more of your stalling," Kathleen said with determination.

Annie raised one eyebrow in my direction after Kathleen walked inside the Iron, but I just shrugged. I knew that we were on delicate ground here and that we both had to watch our steps if we had any hope at all of ensuring domestic harmony in our little family.

⊷⊷⊷⊷⊷

Annie started to produce her copy of the letter, but before Kathleen could grab it, my twin said, "Don't be upset by what you read here. Chester was close to both of us. He trusted us because he knew us so well. I'd like to first tell you what we've been doing since we got this, if you'll allow it."

"Sorry, but my patience is all gone," Kathleen answered as she plucked Annie's letter out of her hands.

"Hey, that's rude," Annie protested.

"File a complaint with the department," she said as she pulled the letter out of its envelope. Kathleen quickly scanned its contents, pausing at the list of suspects Chester had added as an addendum, and then she returned to the main body of the letter. I wanted to say something, and Annie looked as though she were about to burst from holding it in, but to our credit, we both remained silent until she finished. With a frown, Kathleen stared at the letter for a few moments longer, and then she folded the letter back up, returned it to the envelope that it had come in, and put it in her back pocket.

"Hey, that's mine," Annie said.

"Sorry, but I need this."

I was suddenly glad that I hadn't told Kathleen that we had two copies of that letter. Annie clearly didn't care. She wanted hers back, and I could see that she was about to pursue it when I put a hand on her arm. This wasn't the battle that we needed to fight, if only I could make Annie see that.

Was Kathleen disappointed when our sister didn't put up a fight? Maybe, just a little. After she saw that she wasn't going to get a rise out of either one of us, she said, "Now tell me what you know. Start from the beginning, and don't leave anything out, no matter how small or inconsequential it might seem to either one of you."

I looked at Annie. "Do you want to start, or should I?"

"Go ahead," she said, and I started to bring Kathleen up to date on what we'd been doing. Annie interrupted enough so that it was truly coming from both of us, but if our big sister minded, she didn't say anything. We told her everything, including the latest suspicions Lydia and Franklin had shared with her at the grill, but I made it a point to leave out my pending conversation with Harper and hoped that Annie would pick up on it and leave it out as well. By the time we were finished, Kathleen whistled softly under her breath. "I have to give you both credit. You've been busy."

"What could we do, given Chester's request?" I asked her. "We weren't trying to step on your toes, but you can see where we had to do something."

"I can see that you both believe that's true," Kathleen said.

"Is that it? Aren't you going to scold us and tell us to butt out?" Annie asked, pressing our older sibling harder than I would have liked.

Kathleen didn't get upset, though. Instead, she simply

shrugged before she spoke. "You've both done good work here. I already had most of this information, but I'm willing to admit that you've added some valuable tidbits into the mix."

"So then you won't have a problem if we keep working on the case?" Annie asked, clearly as surprised by Kathleen's reaction as I'd been.

"I wouldn't go that far," the sheriff said. "I can't officially endorse what either one of you has done regarding Chester's murder investigation."

"How about unofficially?" I asked her before Annie could get a single word out of her mouth. Now was the time for diplomacy, and I meant to do everything in my power to make it happen.

"No comment," she said, and then our older sister headed for the front door.

"Thanks," I said. "You won't regret it."

"Regret what?" she asked me. "Just promise me one thing, Pat."

"I'll do it if I can," I said.

"Don't do anything stupid or let our sister get herself into more trouble than she can get herself out of, okay?"

Funny, I was the one who was about to do something reckless, not Annie, but I couldn't very well bring that up. "I'll try," I said with a grin, hiding what I could.

"Don't worry. I'm not expecting miracles."

"I'm still here. You both know that, right?" Annie asked plaintively.

"I'm sure that I'll see you both later," Kathleen said, and then she was gone.

"I didn't appreciate that last bit even a little," Annie said as we both did our parts in closing up the Iron for the night. We had half an hour before I had to leave, so I knew that I'd have to hustle to get to the park in time to meet Harper.

"I couldn't very well correct her," I said. "Sorry about that."

"You're forgiven," Annie said a little too easily. "I still don't like the idea of you meeting Harper in the park alone."

"Tell you what. I'll call you the second I leave," I said, trying my best to reassure her. I was beginning to have second thoughts about the wisdom of the meeting myself, but I knew that I couldn't back out now. No matter what happened, I had to continue with my plan. "Is that good enough?"

"No, but it's probably all that I'm going to get, so I'll take it," Annie said as she worked at shutting down her station for the night. Thank goodness we had a dishwasher in the backroom. Otherwise, my twin sister and I would both be up to our elbows in bubbles long past the time for my rendezvous. As it was, I knew that if I didn't hurry at finishing up my closing tasks, I wasn't going to make it.

I finally wrapped things up, though. "Can you finish the rest of this on your own?" I asked Annie. "I really have to go."

"Take off. Remember, you need to be careful, Pat. She might be a killer, so don't ever forget it."

"I won't," I said, and on impulse, I kissed her cheek. "Thanks for worrying about me."

"Hey, it's what I do," she said with a smile, but I could see the worry in her gaze as she said it.

CHAPTER 20: ANNIE

I couldn't believe that my idiot brother took my pledge not to interfere at face value! Frankly, I was a little disappointed in him. It was almost as though he didn't even know me. Of course I was going to follow him to his meeting with Harper. If I didn't and something happened to him, I'd never be able to forgive myself.

I had to be sly about it, though. He knew my car all too well, and if he spotted me in his rearview mirror, I'd be busted. I had an advantage over most tails, though.

I knew where my target was headed.

It took every last ounce of willpower not to speed to catch up with Pat, no matter how little sense that made. My first instinct was to protect my brother, and if that meant that we scared off a potential ally, then so be it. Finally, I had to force myself to pull over into the Shrewsbury's grocery store parking lot. I was going to give Pat five minutes to get to the park and make it to the bench in question, and then I was going after him.

What I didn't count on was running into one of our other suspects while I was there waiting.

I was so absorbed watching the clock on my dashboard that the tap on my window nearly stopped my heart.

"Annie, do you have a second?"

It was Julia Crane, Chester's ex-wife.

"I'm supposed to pick Pat up soon, but I have a minute," I said as I got out of my car. "What's up?"

"I just realized that I had an alibi after all when you asked me about it at Lydia's house yesterday," she said.

"What makes you think I was asking you for an alibi?" I asked, doing my best to deny something that would be patently obvious to anyone who cared to think about it.

"Come on, there's no reason for you to lie about it," she said. "Why wouldn't folks suspect me? I was married to Chester for years, and our breakup wasn't all that pleasant. Then I started dating his biggest rival, and you weren't the first person to suggest that I was getting back at Chester by going out with Bryson."

"Were you?" I asked, honestly interested in what her answer might be.

"At first, there may have been a hint of it in the relationship, but I find myself honestly attracted to Bryson in his own right. Oh, I know he's not much to look at, but he's the first man in a long time that I've ever been with who actually listens to me when I talk. It's quite refreshing. Chester had his moments as well. Actually, the two of them were more alike than either man would have ever admitted; they were both driven to win, whether it was a sale or a woman's heart. Anyway, I was just here to pick up my medication from the pharmacy when I saw you sitting here, so I thought I'd come over and talk to you."

I really wanted her alibi, but this was too good to pass up. "I know that it's none of my business, but do you mind if I ask what kind of meds you're on?"

She looked surprised by my question. "I don't see what it could hurt, though I'm puzzled why you'd want to know. It's nothing very exciting. I've got hypertension. It runs in my family, so I've been on these meds forever."

"Is your medication *just* for high blood pressure?" I asked her, remembering what Lydia had told me earlier about Julia's schizophrenia.

She laughed at the question. "I see that my former sister-in-law has been filling your head with nonsense. She claims I'm on meds because I'm crazy, even though I've repeatedly denied it. Not that there's anything wrong with getting help from medication for whatever ails you, as far as I'm concerned. Mental health is just not an issue with me, but if it were, I wouldn't hide it. Sick is sick, as far as I'm concerned."

I believed her, and while I realized that I might be proven wrong later, for now, her word was good enough for me. "About that alibi, if you'd still like to share it with me, I'd love to hear it."

"It was the darnedest thing," she said with a laugh. "My neighbor's dog has been getting out of their fenced yard, and a little before six on the morning of Chester's murder, I heard something digging in the flowerbeds outside my bedroom window. I threw on a robe to see what was going on, and there was Barkley, digging his way to China and ruining my flowers in the process. Curtis came by as I was trying to stop him, and the second his dog spotted him, Barkley took off like a shot. We chased that dog all the way through the neighborhood, and by the time we finally cornered him, it was well after six thirty. It completely slipped my mind when we were chatting, but I thought it might be important to tell you. Would you mind passing the information on to your sister as well? She was curious about where I was, too."

"I'd be happy to, but it might be better if she heard it from you directly."

"You're probably right. I'll stop by the station and tell her on my way home. See you later."

"Bye," I said as I started my car and headed for the park. The conversation had taken considerably longer than the minute I'd hoped to wait, but I'd been able to garner some pretty valuable information. We were now officially down to four suspects.

I just hoped that I hadn't missed any altercations between Harper and Pat.

When I got to a parking spot near the lake, I couldn't just walk the loop trail to where Pat and Harper were sitting. I had to be a little more stealthy about it, so I started ducking in and out of the woods, doing my best to keep my presence unnoticed. At least there were trees nearby, so I had some shelter from their gazes. I was getting close to them when I saw Harper frown and reach into her oversized handbag.

Was she going to try to strike my brother down as well?

"Pat, look out!" I shouted on impulse as I raced toward them.

Both my brother and Harper looked confused by my sudden appearance, and then, in almost the exact same instant, they both got angry.

"You said that you were here alone!" Harper yelled as she stood.

"I was supposed to be!" Pat shouted right back. "What are you doing here, Annie?"

"She was reaching into her bag," I said, pointing at her as I spoke.

"For lip balm," she protested. "I can't believe you people. Chester told me that I could trust you, but I can see now that he was wrong."

As she angrily started back for her car, Pat tried to follow. "Harper, I didn't know she was there. I swear it."

"Does it even matter at this point?" Harper asked. "I'm not sure that I'll ever be able to believe either one of you now." Pat continued to follow her when she turned abruptly and faced him. "Stop following me, or I'll call the police!"

She'd be calling our sister to stop my brother, but if the irony of that didn't get to her, I wasn't about to point it out. I put a hand on Pat's shoulder. "You need to just let her go."

"Annie, what were you thinking? She was just about to tell me something."

"I'm sorry. I thought she was going to stab you or something."

Pat frowned as he studied me for a moment, and then he hung his head. "You should have trusted me when I said that I could handle things here."

"You're right. The next time, I will. I promise." I wasn't sure that I could keep that pledge, not when my brother's life might be on the line, but at least I was sincere when I said it.

"Okay. I don't suppose there's any way that we can repair this now. Maybe if we give her a little time, she'll come around," he finally said, reluctantly accepting my promise but most likely knowing that there was no way that I was going to be able to keep it. "What happens now?"

"Why don't we go to Glory Landing and track down Nathan Pepper? I'm dying to know if he will substantiate Bryson's alibi."

"Since we've already spoken with Lydia, Franklin, and Harper this afternoon, I suppose it makes sense to dig more into Bryson and Julia."

"Not so fast. It turns out that Julia's off the hook." I brought him up to speed as we made our way to our vehicles.

"So she's in the clear," Pat said as he got out his truck keys. "Good work."

"She found me. All I did was sit there and listen. It was just plain dumb luck," I admitted. "Why don't you drive, and we'll pick my car up later."

"Are you sure?" Pat knew that I liked driving when we went places together, so it was a major concession on my part to allow him to chauffeur me.

"Positive," I said.

He nodded. "Okay. Thanks. Let's go. We can't stay long, though."

How could he possibly know that I was meeting Rob back at my property later? Had the attorney told my brother about our plans? "Why is that?" I asked as coyly as I could manage.

"The park closes at sunset, so if we don't get your car in time, it's going to be locked up here all night," he said. "Why else would we have to rush back?"

"That's the only reason as far as I'm concerned," I said, praying that my brother would drop it. To my delight, that's exactly what he did, and thirty minutes later, we were rolling into Glory Landing in search of a man named Nathan Pepper.

———⋄◇⋄———

Three dead ends later, we were leaving Glory Landing, utterly defeated in our attempts to find Nathan Pepper. We'd left our phone numbers—both personal and the one at the Iron—but I wasn't positive that Nathan would ever get our message. Most likely, we'd have to come back tomorrow to look for him. It was the first real roadblock our investigation had encountered, and as Pat and I drove back to Maple Crest, I found myself envying our older sister's ability to compel folks to speak with her.

"Is there anyone else we need to speak with this evening?" Pat asked me as we neared our hometown.

I wasn't about to tell him about my pending meeting with Rob. "If it's all the same to you, it's been a long day. I'd just as soon pick up my car, run home, and get something to eat. You're welcome to come along, if you'd like." *Please say no, please say no,* I kept repeating in my mind as some kind of mantra as I waited for his reply.

"If you don't mind, I think I'll go it alone tonight," he replied, and it was all I could do not to smile. "Unless you don't want to be by yourself. If that's the case, then I'd be happy to come over." Blast it all, leave it to my brother to be too nice about it.

"No, that's okay. I know how you feel about my driveway at night. Besides, we don't have to spend every waking moment together, do we?"

"No ma'am," he agreed.

As he dropped me off, I was happy to see that Harper hadn't come back to vandalize my car, so I had that going for me, at least. As I got out, I said, "We'll tackle the case again tomorrow."

"You bet we will," Pat said. I got in, and we drove off in tandem, him in front, me in back. We parted ways soon enough, and I headed back home. I had to neaten things up a little if I was going to give the attorney a tour of my place, and if I was lucky, I'd manage to get a bite or two in as I worked.

But only if he wasn't early.

Just my luck, the attorney was already there when I drove up, so that plan was out the window. It looked as though Rob was going to see how I really lived, mess and all.

"You're early," I said as I got out of my car and approached him as he leaned against one of the timber roof supports for my porch.

"Sorry," he said with a grin that told me that he wasn't repentant at all. "I couldn't help myself. I hope you don't mind. I've hiked around a little. I love the pond."

"Thanks. I do, too." With his level of enthusiasm, it was hard to be angry with him. "I'll warn you right now, the cabin's a real mess inside."

"I don't mind. I've been dying to see it." He crowded me a little as I put my key in the lock, and I could almost feel his hot breath on my neck. I'd been attracted to the attorney initially, but there was something a little unsettling about the way he was hovering so close to me now. Had I made a mistake inviting him out to my secluded home without anyone else being there? I hoped not.

After I unlocked the front door and we both went inside, I put a little space between us. If he tried something now, I wasn't sure how I'd defend myself. Looking around, I realized that grabbing the shotgun I kept by the door would look like a severe overreaction, especially if his motives were innocent. Then again, I didn't want to take too much for granted, so I settled on a walking staff I kept by the door for my forays into the woods.

That turned out to be a mistake, though.

"What's that?" he asked as he tried to take it away from me.

"It's my walking stick. Sometimes I like to carry it around inside the cabin." That wasn't even a very good lie. The attorney had me rattled, and not in a good way.

"May I?" he asked politely, withdrawing his grip.

What choice did I have? Feeling like a fool, I surrendered my only weapon. He studied the old man's face I'd carved into it. "This is nice work. Where did you get it?"

"I made it myself," I admitted.

One eyebrow rose. "Really? It's nicely done."

"I think so," I said as I reclaimed it. Somehow, I felt a little better having it back in my possession. "Anyway, this is it. The kitchen's over there, along with the shower, this is the living room, and my sleeping loft is upstairs."

His gaze went up to my bedroom. "I'd love to see that, too," he said as he started toward the ladder.

I put a hand on his shoulder. Something in my gut was telling me not to let him up there. "I'd really rather you didn't. Like I said, it's a mess."

"I don't mind," he said, pulling away from my grasp.

"But I do," I said flatly.

I finally got through to him. Rob stopped in his tracks and pivoted to face me. "Annie, did I do something wrong?"

"If you ask me, you're acting a little too eager," I admitted. "It's creeping me out a little." There, I'd said it.

He shook his head slightly. "Sorry. I just haven't seen a layout like this before. Everything's perfect, from the pond to the woods to the cabin itself." He reached into his front pocket, and I gripped the walking stick tighter. It would do me no good against a gun, but if he had a knife, I liked my chances. There was no way that the attorney's reach could exceed the one I had with my walking stick.

To my surprise though, he pulled out not a weapon but a checkbook. "I've seen enough. Name your price."

I looked at him carefully, the confusion not feigned at all. "Excuse me?"

"I want it. Everything. How much?" he asked as he began scribbling in his checkbook.

"It's not for sale," I said. "If I gave you the impression that it was, I'm sorry."

"Nonsense. Everything is for sale. Just give me a number."

"I think it's time for you to go," I said as I headed for the door.

He didn't follow me. Instead, Rob had this incredulous look on his face. "Annie, there's no sense in doing this dance. I'm hooked. Take advantage of me and name a crazy price you'll take for the place. Who knows? I might just surprise you."

"Sorry, but it's not going to happen. Now, if you don't mind, I've got to neaten things up. My sister, the sheriff, is coming by any minute, and she hates it when my place is a mess." That was a complete and utter lie. Not the part about Kathleen not liking me being messy, but as far as I knew, my big sister had no plans to come out to the cabin that evening or any other. Rob didn't know that, though.

"Okay. I understand," he said as he put his checkbook away. "I handled this all wrong. I can see that now. It's just that I rarely get excited about things these days, and your property is everything I've ever dreamed of owning some day. Annie, when I see something I want, I tend to go after it, full steam ahead." After a moment's pause, he added, "It's kind of like the way I felt about you from the moment I first saw you. Can you find it in your heart to forgive me?"

Rob began to approach me again as he made his request for absolution. Was this fool seriously going to try to kiss me? Why wasn't I using the stick in my hands to fend him off? The least I should have done was take a step back, but I felt as though I was frozen in place.

Was I actually going to let him kiss me after what had just happened?

Whatever spell I'd been under was suddenly broken by my cell phone's ring.

It was my twin, but I didn't want Rob to know that.

"Sorry, but I've got to get this. It's important. Kathleen, could you hold on a second? You're on your way? Okay, I'll see you soon."

Pat was still protesting on his end as I ended the call. "I'm sorry, but I really do need for you to go," I said.

"I understand," Rob said. He was clearly disappointed that he hadn't gotten anything that he'd come for tonight, but that was too bad. I made myself a promise not to let myself get caught alone with him again. He seemed to have some kind of special power over me.

I walked him to his car, and then I made sure that he actually left before I dialed my brother's cell number.

"Sorry about that," I said.

"Since when did I start sounding like Kathleen?" he asked.

"You don't, but I needed someone to think that's who was

calling me," I said. "I'll explain everything later. What's going on with you?"

"Nothing much. I just wanted to see if you wanted to grab a bite with me after all."

"Thanks, but I'm kind of beat," I said. "If you don't mind, I'm just going to stay here at the cabin tonight. You're welcome to leftovers if you feel like trekking out here again."

"Tempting, but no thanks. It was just a thought."

My brother sounded lonely, and I felt bad about turning his offer down so cavalierly. "You know what? I changed my mind. Where would you like to go?"

"Nice try, but I know a pity offer when I hear it," he said with a slight chuckle. "Forget I even called. Have a good night, Annie. I'll see you in the morning."

"Are you sure? I really don't mind," I said.

"I'm positive. We'll talk again soon."

After he hung up, I was tempted to go into town anyway. I had a feeling my brother was feeling sad about Molly's declaration. On impulse, I hit redial.

"Hey, long time no hear," he said.

"Are you sure you wouldn't like to get a bite with me?" I asked him.

He laughed. "I love you like a sister, but I'll be fine on my own."

"I am your sister, you doof," I said, repeating my part in the longstanding joke we shared.

"Good night, Annie."

"Night," I said. I'd made the offer. It was the most that I could do. I started to clean up my cabin's interior, but I quickly got bored with that. After eating some reheated leftovers and reading a little, I headed off to bed.

Fifteen minutes later, I climbed down the ladder again and double-checked the locks on the front door.

After all, in these trying times, a girl couldn't be too careful.

On my way back up to my loft, I grabbed the shotgun and took it with me. If anyone tried to surprise me tonight, they'd get the most unpleasant surprise of their life.

CHAPTER 21: PAT

A FTER I HUNG UP WITH Annie for the second time in two
minutes, I had to laugh out loud about what a big baby I
was being. Normally I loved my single life, living by myself,
eating whatever I wanted whenever I wanted, and staying up as
late as I felt like it watching anything that struck my fancy. Then
there were the times like I was going through at the moment,
where all I felt was lonely. It would pass, and what's more, I
knew it, but that didn't make it any easier getting through those
moments of gentle despair. On the dark evenings when I was lost
in my own thoughts, they always seemed to return to Molly and
what I'd missed out on. I'd always thought that there would be
time for us to work things out, to finally get things right so that
we could be together, but now, apparently, that was no longer
a possibility, and the reality of it was that it made me sad. I
decided that the best thing I could do for my blues was to give
in and wallow in them, at least for the rest of the night. Going
through my movie collection, I found the saddest love story I
had and put it in the machine. Before I hit the play button, I
decided to make a sandwich first, so after I ate a pretty mundane
meal, I settled in for the night. I would never tell either of my
sisters what I was doing, but guys have feelings, too, and this
was exactly what I needed.

Ten minutes into the movie, my doorbell rang. It was rigged
up in back to ring in my apartment above the store, and mostly
only folks who knew me realized that it was even there. I hit the

pause button, and for one second, I found myself hoping that it was Molly, there to tell me that she'd changed her mind and that she wanted to be with me forever. I nearly tripped going down the stairs, I was so excited.

When I got there, it wasn't Molly after all.

To my surprise, it was Harper Gentry.

The look of disappointment on my face must have been pretty evident. "Hi," I said as I opened the door for her.

"Were you expecting someone else, Pat?" she asked. "I can come back later if you'd like."

"I'm surprised you're here at all after what you said earlier."

"I couldn't very well stay away from the Iron forever, could I?" she asked. "Whether I like it or not, this place is the central nervous system for the entire town."

"I'm glad you came. That wasn't what I was talking about, though. What happened at the park really wasn't my fault. My sister was worried about me. That's all that it was."

"Was she honestly afraid that I might do something to you?" Harper asked as she stepped in and I closed the door behind her. I wasn't at all sure that Annie would approve of this meeting, but I couldn't let my sister's paranoia rule my actions. Besides, why would Harper want to hurt me? I knew that Annie and I had discussed the possibility that whoever had killed Chester might be coming after us next, but without any apparent motivation, I was having a hard time giving the theory any credence.

"She has a right to worry about me. It's the whole twin thing," I said. "If you'd like to come upstairs, I can make us some coffee."

"Would you mind?" she asked. "I didn't mean to interrupt your evening."

"You aren't," I answered. "I was just settling in for an old movie."

"I love movies. What were you going to watch?"

I told her the title, and then she said, "That makes me so sad."

"What, that I'm watching a tear jerker by myself?" I asked her with the hint of a smile.

"No, the movie itself. It's absolutely tragic, isn't it?"

"Most love stories seem to end that way," I said. Wow, I really was in a somber mood.

Harper didn't disagree with me. "I won't keep you long. I've been thinking about Chester, and there are a few things that I'd like to talk to you about."

"Come on up," I said as I led the way up the stairs, through the storage area, and into my apartment.

"I wasn't prepared for this. It is really nice," she said as she took in my living space.

"What did you expect, an attic?" I asked her, smiling again. There was something about Harper that made me want to impress her, and if I couldn't do that, I would at least like to be entertaining.

"No, but this is really quite cozy," she said as she took her jacket off.

I headed for my little kitchen and started a pot of coffee. She took a seat at my small banquette, and I put a few cookies on a plate and offered them to her. "Sorry it's not something nicer."

"These are fine," she said as she took one and nibbled on it. "First of all, let me say that I'm sorry I overreacted at the lake earlier. I panicked a little when your sister came out of the trees like that."

"It just about gave me a heart attack, too," I confessed. "I had no idea she was lurking in the shadows."

"You really didn't, did you?" Harper asked me.

"Hey, I make it a policy never to lie if I can help it."

"That's rather honorable of you," she said.

"Really, I've just found that honesty is easier. That way I don't have to remember any of the lies I've told, so there's nothing to keep straight."

She surprised me by laughing at that. "I never looked at it that way."

"Feel free to adopt it yourself. Whenever you're ready to talk, I've been told that I am a very good listener."

"I have no trouble believing that," Harper said, and then she frowned. "There are a few things Chester told me within the last week that have me on edge. I wanted to tell someone, and you were the first person that came to mind."

"I'm flattered," I replied. "What did he say?" I asked as I served us both coffee.

"It's about his brother and sister," Harper said. "I'm a little reluctant to share this with anyone else, but if something should happen to me, no one will ever know."

"Has there been an attempt on your life, too?" I asked her.

"No, at least not so far. Still, I'm being really careful until Chester's killer is caught."

"What did you want to share with me? Go on. It's all right. You can tell me."

She frowned for a moment. "He thought they were up to something, but he couldn't prove anything."

"Did he happen to mention anything more specific than that?"

She bit her lower lip for a few moments before she spoke. It was clear that she was having trouble sharing with me, and I did my best not to do anything to dissuade her from it. After another moment or two, she continued.

"Chester ordered a new safe for the house. Did you know about that?"

My sister had overheard something about it, but I decided to play dumb. "Why did he feel that he needed one?"

"When their mother died, Chester, Franklin, and Lydia were dividing up the assets. Franklin and Lydia took their share in cash, but Chester chose his mother's jewelry instead. It had more than sentimental value to him, and that's just the way that he was. Lydia seemed okay with it at the time, but when she blew through her share of the inheritance, she started claiming that Chester had cheated her. She demanded a third of the jewelry, even though she wasn't entitled to any of it, and Chester flatly refused. She said if she had to, she'd break in and steal her share back herself, and Chester never took her threats lightly, so he ordered a new safe."

"Where are the jewels now?"

She shrugged. "They must still be in his smaller safe, as far as I know. You might want to ask your sister about that. If any of them are gone, I'd look harder at Lydia."

This was interesting, and it added a new motive for Chester's sister if it were true. I had more questions for Harper though, since she was in such a talkative mood. "Is there anything else?"

She nodded. "Chester had a few close calls recently, one with a car and the other with a gun."

"I know all about both of those events," I said as I poured the coffee the moment the percolator shut off.

"You do?" She seemed surprised by the admission.

"Chester told Annie and me," I said, not getting into the details of the letter and its codicils. I wanted to keep this a fact-finding mission and not a fact-sharing one.

"That's good to hear. I was hoping that he'd talk to someone about them, and I'm glad that he chose you and your sister," she said. "Anyway, he kept wondering if Franklin or Lydia might be behind the accidents. They were both under the impression that they were the main beneficiaries of his will, so it's not entirely outside the realm of possibility that one of them decided to speed things up."

"As far as you know, are the two of them going to inherit anything?" I asked. I knew that Franklin and Lydia were going to get twenty-five percent of the estate each and that Julia and Harper were getting ten percent cuts, but what I really needed to know was if Harper was aware of the details of the will herself.

"I don't know anything about that, and Chester didn't tell me," she admitted. "The will has been sealed until a week after he's been cremated, so we won't know for sure for several days. As things stand right now, only his attorney knows, and he's not saying. That's my next point, actually."

"What's that?"

"Chester was beginning to wonder about Robert Benton. I'm not entirely certain that he trusted him anymore."

I knew that Chester had been ambivalent about his attorney from the letter we'd received, so Harper was just confirming what we'd read in the dead man's missive. "Did he happen to say why not?"

"I couldn't get him to admit anything more than that," she said. "You know how Chester was. His left hand didn't know what his right hand was doing half the time, and I didn't feel right about pressuring him for more information."

"I understand that," I said. "I'm just not sure what I can do about it."

She put her coffee cup down on the table and looked directly into my eyes. "I'm not at all certain, either. Chester said that I could trust you, though, and that I should help you in any way that I could. I'm doing that right now, based solely on his instructions."

"I'm beginning to think that he gave us more credit than we deserve," I admitted.

"Just don't forget about him," she said, and I could see tears beginning to form in her eyes before she quickly brushed them away. "And don't let your older sister put it on the back burner until no one cares anymore."

"Trust me, that's not going to happen," I said as I patted her hand. "Did he implicate anyone besides his siblings to you?"

She frowned for a moment, and then Harper said, "The truth was that he was also worried about Bryson and Julia. I don't know if he was just being paranoid, but he thought the two of them might be conspiring together to hurt him."

"Why would they do that?"

"I'm not sure, but what if Chester never changed his will? He was married to Julia at one time, so greed could be a motive for her as well if she inherits the lion's share of his estate. As for Bryson, he was always upset that Chester was a better businessman than he was. He had motives of his own."

"Those two are in the clear," I told her, instantly regretting my words.

She perked up at the news. "Seriously? How can you know?"

"Until we learn any differently, they both have alibis for the time of the murder," I confessed, "but I don't know much beyond that." In truth, I really didn't. In fact, I'd just given one of my suspects valuable information about two other people who had aroused our suspicions. Wow, I really did have a lot to learn about investigating murder.

Did she look a little disappointed when I told her the news? I couldn't really tell, but I believed that I'd seen something in her eyes for one brief moment. Maybe she'd wanted Chester's ex-wife to be his killer. If she did, the reaction was perfectly understandable. "That's good, then, isn't it? It narrows the field quite a bit."

Was she actually including herself in the list of suspects? I was about to ask her to clarify what she meant when she added,

"Based on what Chester told me, it has to be either Lydia, Franklin, or Robert Benton."

"I'm still not convinced that the attorney should be included in the list," I said. "What possible motive could he have had? I doubt that he'll gain anything by Chester's death."

"Unless there's something motivating him besides greed," she suggested.

"I'm willing to admit that I might be wrong about him, but I do agree that Lydia and Franklin should be looked at closely."

"Do they have alibis of their own, do you know?"

"I believe my sister is still looking into them," I answered. It wasn't exactly a lie. At least that's what I told myself.

"Alibis are funny things, aren't they?" she asked me.

"How so?"

"I would think that only the guilty people would have them."

"I'm not sure that it's that simple," I said. "It's perfectly reasonable for most folks to have a corroborating witness to their location without it causing any suspicion."

"At six in the morning?" she asked. "I know I don't have anyone who could prove that I was home alone, asleep. Does that make me a suspect in your mind, or not?"

"Until we unmask who killed Chester, everyone is a suspect from my point of view," I said firmly.

"Even me?"

I shrugged my shoulders slightly and offered her a brief smile. "Even you. I hope you don't take it personally."

"I'll try not to," she said, answering with a slight grin of her own. Harper was closer to my age than Chester's, and if I hadn't been so hung up on Molly, I might have considered asking her out in the past. Maybe some time in the future, after she had a chance to get over losing Chester and my heart had a little time to heal, there might be something there to pursue.

A moment later, Harper stood. "Well, I've taken up enough of your time. I just had to get that off my chest."

"I appreciate you stopping by. Let me walk you out."

"Thanks, but I can manage on my own," she said as she started for the stairs.

"I insist," I said with a smile, and I followed her to the back entrance, let her out, and then locked the Iron up again for the night.

I wondered what Annie would make of my conversation with Harper. I could wait and tell her in the morning, but then I decided to give her a call immediately. If she was sleeping, her ringer would be off, so there was no danger in waking her.

As I suspected, her ringer was off, and my call went straight to voicemail. I hung up without going into any detail in a message and decided that I'd bring her up to speed in the morning.

When I turned the movie back on, I found that I'd lost all interest in the interim, so I shut everything down and called it an early evening myself.

Detecting, I was discovering, was getting to be a tiring process.

I couldn't imagine how Kathleen did it on a full-time basis, and I realized that I was discovering a whole new level of respect for my big sister.

CHAPTER 22: ANNIE

"**B**EFORE YOU GET MAD AT what I'm about to tell you, at least give me a chance to explain first," my brother Pat told me the next morning when I came into the Iron bright and early. He'd been up for a while from the look of things, and something was most definitely on his mind.

"What did you do?" I asked him as I prepped my workstation at the range.

"I didn't do anything," he said in protest. "Well, I suppose if you look at it one way, I did, but I didn't see any way around it. Maybe you could have come up with a better way to handle it, but I couldn't."

"Just spit it out, Pat."

"Harper showed up here last night after you left," he said simply.

I counted to six until I could keep my temper in check. As many times as I'd tried in the past to count to ten, I never seemed to make it, so I'd ended up shortening it. "She came here. To the Iron. When you were alone."

"That's right," he said.

"I thought the entire reason you had to meet her at the lake was because she couldn't come back here where Chester was murdered."

"That's what she told me at the time," Pat explained.

"So, what changed in such a short amount of time?"

"She said that since the Iron was such an integral part of the

174

I hadn't had time to comment on that when Skip walked in. He was holding a large box in his arms. "Am I the last one in again? Man, you guys need to learn to take it easy and chill out."

"Is that how you justify coming in late?" my brother asked him with a grin.

"When was two minutes early ever late?" Skip asked him with a smile. "You should see what I've got for my corner today." He found an empty space at the front counter and opened the box. "I'm really pleased with the way these turned out."

Skip was one of the craftiest people I knew, so it was hard to tell what he'd come up with, but chances were that it was at least as good as he was promising. With more flourish than the occasion probably called for, Skip reached into the box and pulled out the first piece, an elegant vase with the most fascinating glaze on it that I'd ever seen. Golds, blues, and greens sparkled as the light hit different parts, and I wondered how he'd managed to come up with such a lovely effect.

"You're right," I said as I took it from him and turned it around and around in my hands. "How did you do that?"

"I have no idea," he said with a grin. "Not really. I have a theory, but I can't check it until Sunday when I'm glazing the next round of my creations. It's really something, isn't it?"

"It is," I said as I tried to hand it back to him.

"Keep it," Skip said with a grin, his face beaming with pride that I'd liked his work.

"I can't do that," I said as I tried to give it back to him again.

"Come on, Annie. Think of it as a present," he insisted.

"How about if I pay for it, but I only give you what I'd pay with our store discount?" I countered.

"I can live with that," Skip said, and I reached into my wallet and paid him seventy percent of the price he'd stickered onto it. "That way we're both happy."

"If you'll excuse me, the day's mail will be here any minute, so I have to get ready for it," Edith said, and she disappeared into her little section of our world, a domain where she had full authority.

"I've got boxes to unpack," Skip said after he restocked the shelf on his own corner.

"There's more?" Pat asked him.

"Not this run. I was talking about the truck from MDP we got in yesterday."

"Good," Pat said. "I'll give you a hand in a minute."

Skip tapped his watch and grinned. "Tick tick tick, boss," he said.

Pat laughed as Skip disappeared in back.

"Where does that leave us with our investigation?" Pat asked me quietly after we were alone again, though I knew that it wouldn't last long.

"Where else? We keep digging into Chester's murder after we close for the day, but if any of our suspects come our way, it wouldn't hurt to take a stab at asking them a few questions. I've got a feeling that if we keep applying pressure, one of them's bound to crack sooner or later."

"The real question is which one, though," I said.

"I wish I knew," Pat said as he headed up front to get his register ready to serve our customers, while I retreated to my grill where I needed to do the same thing.

The first thing I did was whip up some dough for English muffins. They were easier to make than most folks realized, and I loved the hard, crisp crust they developed when I cooked them in a cast iron frying pan on top of the range. They were one of my favorites, so I made enough dough so I could sneak one or two myself if things got slow. As that dough was rising, I got started on the biscuit dough next. After that, it was time to stock my little fridge with eggs, bacon, and other goodies I'd need to have on hand. Once that was all set, I needed to make lunch, so the first thing I did was preheat the oven to just under 300 degrees. I'd gotten a good deal on stew beef, so I browned the meat in some olive oil after coating the pieces in flour, using a couple of my old cast iron Dutch ovens. Next I added broth, water, carrots, potatoes, onions, peas, and spices to the mixtures. After everything was in the pots, I gave it all a good stir to make sure that it was incorporated, and then I added a slurry made from cornstarch and water to thicken the gravy. I poured that mixture on top of each meal, and then I covered the pots with their matching heavy lids and slid them into the oven. Some of my Dutch ovens had legs on them, but I reserved those for cooking outside, like I did in my classes. The flat-bottom ones were perfect for the oven. In four hours, the meals would be ready to eat, and in the meantime, as they simmered away, they would fill the Iron with the homespun aroma of how many of our grandmothers used to cook.

Pat called out to me just as I closed the oven door, "Are we ready to open for the day?"

"You betcha," I said, and he unlocked the front door.

It was time for a little normalcy in our lives, in spite of the murder that had happened so close by. Life did indeed go on, and there was no better way for me to handle things than to fire up my burners, my griddle, and my ovens and feed anyone who happened to wander by.

I served a fair number of people breakfast, but none of them happened to be on our list of suspects. Was it wrong that this made me a little sad? I hadn't even had the chance to sample the English muffins myself. As expected, they'd been a hit with my diners. No worries; I could always make more, something that gave me great comfort.

I was just about to transition from breakfast to lunch, since the stew was finished and ready to serve seven minutes ahead of time, when someone spoke up from behind me. "Excuse me. Are you Annie Marsh, by any chance?"

"I am," I said as I turned to see a rail-thin older man with a large salt-and-pepper mustache looking at me. "How may I help you?"

"Well, I wouldn't say no to a plate of whatever it is that smells so wonderful coming from that oven," he answered with a smile as he took one of the empty seats at the bar.

"I can make that happen. Would you like sweet tea or coffee with your lunch?"

"Tea would be great."

After I dished him up some of the stew and served it, along with his drink, I said, "Surely you didn't come here asking for me by name because of my reputation as a cook."

"That might not have been the original reason that I came in, but if this tastes a third as good as it looks and smells, I'll be back."

"What can I do for you?"

"It's what I can do for you, actually," he said, and then he took a bite. The man lingered over it so long that I was beginning to wonder if everything was all right.

"Is it too heavy on the bay leaves?" I asked him. I tended to like it in stews myself, and sometimes I used a little too much of it for other people's tastes.

"It's perfect. If I didn't know any better, I'd swear that Ruth made this herself."

"Should I be jealous of Ruth?" I asked him with a slight grin. I liked this man. Despite his slender profile, it was clear that he was someone who enjoyed his food, which made him a man after my own heart.

"Sadly, she's been gone seven years come September," he said.

"I'm so sorry."

"Don't be. You made me smile in her honor today, and that's something worth cherishing." He took another bite, and then he said, "I understand you and your brother were looking for me yesterday."

"You're not Nathan Pepper, are you?"

"I am," he said. "And you're looking for an alibi for Bryson Oak, aren't you?"

I hadn't planned on being so obvious about it, but there was no way that I was going to beat around the bush with this man. I liked him too much. "Was he with you?"

"He was indeed," Mr. Pepper said. "I've been making him wine and dine me for a month before I'll sell him property that I want to get rid of for more money than it's worth." He seemed to take a great deal of satisfaction out of that declaration. "You won't tell him I said that, will you?"

I grinned at him before I spoke. "Don't worry. Your secret is safe with me."

He took another bite and then another. "I told the sheriff, and now I'm telling you. Bryson may not be my favorite fellow, but he didn't kill your friend."

"Kathleen was looking for you, too?" I asked him. That was news to me.

"Yes, I got back into town, and half a dozen folks told me that three people were looking for me from Maple Crest, so I thought I'd save you all the trouble of coming back to Glory Landing and find you instead." He took the remnants of his biscuit and dropped it into his nearly empty bowl, and after giving it a few moments, he scooped it up again with his spoon, savoring the liquid-soaked bread. "If I had any room, I'd order another, but I'm about to burst as it is. Don't worry, though. I'll be back now that I know that you're here."

He grabbed his wallet and started to pay me, but I stopped him. "My brother takes the money up front."

"Fair enough," he said as he stood, and then Mr. Pepper polished off the last of his tea and grinned. "Thank you, my dear, for the food as well as for the memories."

"You're most welcome," I said, smiling at the man as he approached my brother and paid for his lunch. Customers like him were what made my job worthwhile, and I hoped to see him again. He'd lightened my load and brightened my day, something I never got enough of.

As I served more stew throughout the rest of our lunchtime, I managed to grab a small bowl for myself, as well as one for Pat, and a pair of biscuits, too. Edith never ate my food, preferring to bring her own from home, and Skip was an enthusiastic, if sporadic customer, but my brother and I always ate our lunches at the Iron, though rarely together. Even after our meal, there was still some stew left by the time we were ready to close for the day, and I delighted in the thought that my brother and I would have leftovers to share.

I was starting to clean the griddle, a task I performed several times over the course of the day, when I saw my sister come in through the front door. She was gnawing on her bottom lip, so I knew that something was troubling her.

I just hoped that it wasn't anything that Pat or I had done.

She said something to my brother, and after he called Skip over to take the front, the two of them approached me in back at my grill.

What on earth was going on now?

CHAPTER 23: PAT

"ANNIE, DO YOU HAVE A second?" I asked my twin as Kathleen and I approached. The sheriff had started to tell me something about the case, but I'd insisted that we include Annie. I didn't even think that Kathleen was all that surprised by my request.

"I'm just cleaning up," Annie said.

"Can it wait?" Kathleen asked.

"You bet it can. Pat, there are only a few stragglers here. Why don't we close up early?"

"I have a better idea," I said. "Put your Closed sign on the bar and I'll have Skip finish checking folks out. That way we can all go upstairs where we'll have a little privacy."

"I'd rather talk on the back porch," Kathleen suggested.

I didn't want to say no to her again. "Even better." After Annie put up her sign, I signaled to Skip that we'd be out back. The three of us stepped through the back door, through the small storage space, and out into the day. Edith had been right; it had been raining for a few hours, and water dripped off the back porch roof in a steady trickle.

Once we were all outside, Kathleen got started. "Did Pepper find you?"

"He did," I said. "Thanks for sending him our way." After he'd told Annie about the alibi, he shared it with me as well, leaving us a substantial tip on his way out, too. I suspected that we hadn't seen the last of him based on the way he had raved about Annie's cooking.

"Good. I asked him to come by. It turns out that Bryson is in the clear, and so is Lydia."

"What?" Annie asked incredulously.

"You sound surprised," Kathleen said.

"That's because she was near the top of our list," I chimed in.

"Why is that?"

"According to one of our sources, Chester suspected her; she wanted his money, not to mention their mother's jewelry."

Kathleen looked at me oddly. "How did you hear about that?"

"What can I say? People talk," I said noncommittally. I was reluctant to tell our older sister where I'd gotten the information. Harper had placed her trust in me, and I saw no reason to name her as my source.

"I bet they do. We still haven't been able to crack open that will yet, but thanks to Chester's letter that you two shared with me, we have a pretty good idea what is in it. The good news is that we found all the jewelry in question in Chester's safe, and Lydia's alibi checks out, too. I was able to confirm it this morning."

"Wow, that was good police work, Kathleen," Annie said.

"Believe it or not, I haven't been sitting around just waiting for you to solve this case for me. Just in case he made your list, too, I was able to clear the attorney, Robert Benton III, as well."

"How did you know that he was among our suspects?" I asked her.

"I didn't know for sure, but he made mine, so I figured there was a good chance you two were looking at him as well. Luckily for him, he was in Atlanta when the murder occurred. Who does that leave on your list?"

"We've still got Harper and Franklin left," I admitted.

"Well, you can forget all about Harper. Franklin did it, as far as I'm concerned."

"Do you have some proof that we don't?" I asked her.

"If you think about it, it's pretty clear that he's the only one left who had the motive, the means, and the opportunity. It's no secret that he and his brother disliked each other in the extreme, and he lied to me about not seeing Chester days before he died. I have an eyewitness who puts them together the night before the murder, just after Chester's argument with Harper. That leaves his greed, and there's no doubt in my mind."

"Was Les your eyewitness to that argument, too?" Annie asked her.

Kathleen looked at her askance. "I'm not even going to ask you how you knew that, but yes, Les was the one who told me. Oh, and Franklin drives a dark-blue Suburban, so he could have easily been the one who tried to run Chester down. My guess is that when that failed, he decided to take a more direct approach with a rifle before he settled on a frying pan."

"We can't even confirm that he was at the Iron the day before the murder," I said. "How could he swipe Annie's pan?"

"Maybe he took it a few days earlier than we first thought," Kathleen said, and then she turned to our sister. "Annie, can you honestly tell me that it wasn't missing until just before the murder? Do you use that pan every day?"

"I think so," she said, and then she looked at me. "Pat, could I have been wrong about that?"

"I don't know, but I'm inclined to doubt it," I said. "Annie, you work with those things every day." I turned to Kathleen. "What about the shooting? Do you have anything concrete about him owning a weapon of his own? And what about his alibi?"

"Just because we can't find any record of him being armed doesn't mean that he's not, and as for the alibi, nobody saw him driving back to Maple Crest. He might as well have claimed to be home in bed alone like a few of my other suspects. No, it's Franklin. I'm sure of it."

"I wish I could be as sure of it as you seem to be," I said.

"Pat, if we wait around for all of our questions to be answered, it may be too late. I'm not about to stand around doing nothing while Franklin takes off for parts unknown. Do me a favor, you two. Stay away from him. He's dangerous, and I don't want you taking any chances. I can't afford to lose either one of you, even if one of you is just a spare." It was an old joke, but she'd made her point.

"We won't go anywhere near Franklin until this is resolved if we can help it," I said.

"Pat, how can you possibly promise that?" Annie asked.

I just shrugged. "We don't have much choice, Annie."

She reluctantly nodded her head. "Okay, I agree."

Kathleen looked more relieved than anything else. "Thank you both. I was afraid that was going to be harder than it turned out to be. Don't worry. I'll let you know when it's all over."

She left, ducking into the rain instead of going through the store to get back to her cruiser.

Annie wasn't ready to go inside just yet, though.

She grabbed my arm before I could move, either. "What was that all about? Why did you force me to make that promise to Kathleen?"

"Because I think she's wrong," I said. "I've been thinking about it, and I believe Harper is the real killer."

CHAPTER 24: ANNIE

"Harper?" I asked Pat. "Really? What makes you think that?"

"Let's consider what we've been able to learn so far," my brother said. "Everyone now knows that Harper had a major argument with Chester the day before he died. Shoot, she even admitted it. She also confessed that she'd come by the Iron earlier that same day, so she could have easily swiped that pan of yours, and lastly, her alibi was that she was home alone. Why couldn't it be her?"

"She drives a red Miata, for one thing," I reminded him.

"That doesn't mean that she couldn't have borrowed someone else's car to take a run at Chester, or even that it might have just been a coincidence," he argued.

"Okay, then how about the gunshots? We can't find any evidence that she's ever fired a gun, let alone owned one."

"This is the South," Pat said. "Need I remind you how many women are taught to shoot at an early age by their fathers? Dad taught you, didn't he? Why should Harper be any different? There's something else, too. She's been awfully interested in discovering what I know about the case, and just as dedicated to feeding me information and speculation about our other suspects."

"She could be doing all of that out of her love for Chester. Her explanation that she wanted to share what Chester told her before something happened to her too could still be valid," I reminded him. "Harper doesn't deny that they had a fight, and the next day he was murdered before she had a chance to make up with him. Isn't that motivation enough for her to do her best to make sure that the killer is caught?"

For the first time, my brother was beginning to look a little unsure about his theory. "I guess you could be right. Maybe I was just blinded by the way she kept seeking me out so she could feed me information about everyone else. Perhaps Kathleen is right after all, and Franklin is the real killer."

"It's possible," I said.

"So, do you honestly think that he might have killed his brother, too?" Pat asked me.

"I'm not ready to say that, but I don't think we should give up on either one of them until we get more information. That's why I didn't want to agree to stay away from Franklin."

"Sorry, Sis. It looks as though I blew it."

I wasn't about to kick my brother when he was down. "If I'd had the same experience with Harper that you'd had, I probably would have felt the same way you did," I said. "We might not be able to approach Franklin, but Kathleen didn't say a word about us talking to Harper again."

"You're right. Let's get the store closed up, and then we'll go see if we can put a little more pressure on her. Who knows? We might just get lucky and make her crack."

"It's worth a shot," I agreed and I turned to go back inside.

Through the rain, I heard something in the woods beside the store, like a stick breaking from a heavy footfall.

Someone was out there; I just knew it.

Was it Franklin or maybe even Harper eavesdropping on our conversation? Or perhaps it had just been a squirrel running through the woods. If it *was* one of our two last suspects, then they knew our game plan, and worse yet, how to thwart us.

I nearly jumped out of my skin when my cell phone rang as

I peered into the rain. I planned to ignore it until I saw that it was Kathleen.

"Hey. Did you get Franklin?"

"We can't find him," she said, sounding nearly out of breath. "You two need to be extremely careful. He's dangerous, and if your theory is right that he has something against the two of you as well, you're both in danger. You need to get away from the Iron as fast as you can right now."

"Do you really think that he'd come after us?" I asked her softly. There was movement in the woods again, but I still couldn't see anything suspicious.

"He killed Chester on your front porch with one of your frying pans for a reason. We just don't know what it is yet."

"Okay, we'll be careful, but we have to close up first, even if he's outside waiting for us."

"Is it worth dying over, Annie?" I didn't think I'd ever heard my sister that agitated before, and it had my nerves on edge.

"We'll be as quick as we can," I said. "Do me a favor and let me know when you find him, would you?"

"Will do."

"What was that all about?" Pat asked me after I hung up.

"Let's go inside first," I said, still trying not to be so obvious as I scanned the woods.

"Now do you want to tell me?" he asked as we walked into the Iron.

I bolted the back door before I spoke. "Did you hear something in the woods just then?"

"I did, but it was probably just a squirrel," he said. "They sound as though they weigh a hundred pounds sometimes. Are you getting jumpy, Sis?"

"Shouldn't we both be on edge?" I asked him. "After all, there's a killer loose in town, and they may want to harm us."

"Who was on the phone? Was it Kathleen?"

"It was," I said. "She can't find Franklin."

Pat took that news in before he spoke. "That doesn't necessarily mean that he's going to come after us next."

"It's not exactly good news either, is it?"

"What does she suggest we do?"

"She told me that we need to get away from the Iron as quickly as we can manage it," I told him.

"That's probably not bad advice," Pat replied.

"Don't tell me you've changed your mind."

He shrugged. "What can I say? We're both new at this. How can we be so sure that we're right about either one of them? I'm going to send Skip home, and then we're going to wrap things up here as quickly as we can. I don't see what possible harm it could do taking Kathleen's advice on this."

"Are you worried?" I asked him.

"You said it yourself. There's a killer roaming the streets, and we may be the next two people on their list."

"Does that mean that you've changed your mind about pressing Harper?"

He sighed. "No, I don't think we have any choice. If Kathleen's right, it won't hurt anything, but if she's wrong, somebody needs to keep an eye on our other suspect."

"Then we have a plan. We finish up here, and then we lock up and go find Harper Gentry."

CHAPTER 25: PAT

I T WAS THE FASTEST WE'D ever closed the Iron, and I had to wonder if Annie hadn't skipped a step or two cleaning up her grill. She was usually diligent in making sure that everything would be ready to use first thing the next morning, but we had something more urgent to do.

As for me, I didn't even bother running our reports or totaling the cash we'd taken in. I decided to do that in the morning, and I jammed the entire till's contents into our safe. "Are you ready?" I asked her after I'd safely stored the money away.

Annie frowned as she looked around her area. "I hate leaving things like this."

"We can always come in early tomorrow," I said. "From what you said, Kathleen was pretty adamant about us getting out of here as soon as possible."

"Between what she said and the feeling I had out back that someone was watching us, I can't get out of here fast enough."

We went out through the front door, locking up behind us, and we headed to the parking area where we kept our vehicles. I decided to bring something up that I'd been thinking about since Kathleen had called my sister. "Annie, should we split up? It will make searching for Harper a lot easier, because we can cover twice as much ground."

"I don't care how much sense it makes, Pat, I don't want to be away from you right now. Do you think I'm being silly?"

"No, you're probably right. It's bound to be safer if we stick together," I said. "Let's take your car. It's not as obvious as my truck is, and besides, if we leave my vehicle parked out here, anyone who comes looking for us will think that at least one of us is still inside."

"How is that to our advantage?" she asked me.

"If the killer thinks that we're here, they won't expect us to be someplace else," I said.

"That makes as much sense as anything else does," Annie answered as we headed for her car.

We drove to Harper's place, but Annie stopped well short of it. "Why are you parking here?" I asked her.

"Well, we can't exactly drive up to her house and knock on the front door, can we?"

"Why shouldn't we do exactly that?" I asked. "After all, we're not accusing her of anything. We're here to ask her some questions. Is there any reason this shouldn't be presented as a normal visit?"

"Probably not," Annie conceded as she started her car again. "I guess I'm still jumping at shadows. You're not armed, are you?"

I looked at her oddly before I answered. "Have you ever known me to carry a weapon around on me?"

"No, but these circumstances are a little different. What if she is the killer and she decides to make a run at us?"

"Well, one thing's certain; neither one of us is about to turn our back on her, so if she comes after us with any sort of weapon, it won't be a sneak attack."

"Just because she may have conked Chester on the back of the head with one of my skillets doesn't mean that she'll try to use the same kind of weapon against us," Annie said.

"Sorry, but I'm not armed. Don't you have anything in your car we can use for protection?"

"Not that I can think of, but feel free to look through the glove box," she said.

I opened it and started rooting around. "Hey, here's the multitool I gave you for Christmas two years ago." It was a combination set of pliers, a file, screwdrivers, small knives, and a few other doodads, all presented in one tool.

"Sorry I haven't used it yet," she said. "I've been meaning to take it out of the car, but I keep forgetting."

"Right now, I'm glad that you didn't," I said as I started unfolding the tool and opening the largest knife within it. It was only three inches long, but it was the best that we could do on such short notice. "Take this. You might need it," I said as I folded the knife back into the handle.

"What are you going to use?" she asked me as she took it.

I tapped my temple and grinned at her. "I'll think of something. After all, I'm the brains of the operation, remember?"

"Pat, this isn't the time to be funny."

"I know," I said, "but don't worry about me. If things get rough, I've got you to protect me."

Annie tucked the multitool into her pocket, and we drove all the way up Harper's drive.

Once we got out of the car, I said, "Here goes nothing," and we approached the front door.

There was only one problem, though.

She wasn't home.

———————⊷⊙◇⊙⊶———————

"What do we do now?" Annie asked me.

"You go that way, and I'll go this way," I suggested. "There's got to be a chance that she's around back." At least the rain had finally stopped.

"What happened to us sticking together?" Annie asked me.

"We're not driving off in separate directions. We need to split up for just a minute to make sure she doesn't sneak up on us. Don't worry. Everything will turn out fine."

"Okay, but be careful," Annie said.

"See you in a minute," I said.

Annie took off in one direction, and I headed in the other. If Harper was outside instead of in the house, one of us would run into her soon enough, and the other would be there soon, coming from the other direction for backup.

At least that was our plan.

It was too bad that it didn't work out that way.

When I got to the side door, I decided that it wouldn't hurt anything to peek inside. As I approached, though, I was startled when it opened suddenly, and our murder suspect was standing much too close to me for my own comfort.

"Pat, what are you doing creeping around outside my house?" Harper asked me critically. She was toweling off her hair, and her clothes looked fresh.

"In my defense, I rang your bell first," I said. I didn't want to give away the fact that my twin was there with me, so I vowed to keep using the singular instead of the plural.

"Sorry. I didn't hear you. I was in the shower."

Had she *really* been taking a shower, or was her hair wet from lurking outside the Iron in the rain? Maybe Annie had been right about someone eavesdropping on our conversation after all. If so, Harper had to know that we suspected her of murdering her boyfriend.

"If this is a bad time, I can always come back later," I said as I took a step back. Where was Annie? I needed her to know what was going on, but I was still hoping that she'd stay undetected.

"No, now is fine. Come on in."

"Honestly, I don't mind postponing our conversation until

later." If I was lucky and she really had been showering, maybe I still had a chance to get away.

That's when I looked up and saw the kitchen knife in Harper's hands.

"Get in here right now," she ordered.

Apparently the last bit of my luck had just run out.

⁂

It took every ounce of willpower I had not to shout out to Annie to run. If Harper knew that my sister was close by, it might spell trouble for my twin as well, and at the very least, we'd lose the element of surprise, which was about the only thing that we had going for us at the moment. I cursed myself silently for not being armed when I started to comply and walk into the house. For an instant, I considered turning and running away, but how fast was Harper with that knife? And what if I escaped, but she managed to hurt Annie instead? I knew that I couldn't live with myself if that happened. No, it was better to do as I was told and hope that my sister would be able to get help before Harper finished me off. I intentionally took my time obeying her command, however.

Harper wasn't having any of that, though.

"Come on, Pat. The longer you wait, the worse it's going to be for you, and your entire family, too."

That was it. I knew that I had to move. There was still hope that I could help Annie, though. As I walked in, I noticed that the side-door lock was one of those old-fashioned push-button models. It was set to lock when it closed, but I might be able to do something about that. I pretended to trip on the sill as I stepped inside and banged against the door for a moment. As I righted myself, I pushed the button and coughed loudly to cover the noise of what I'd done.

"Let's go! I'm losing my patience with you," she said as she moved the knife closer to my chest.

"Sorry. I tripped," I said.

Harper closed the door, and I held my breath, praying that she wouldn't see what I'd done. It appeared that she'd missed it! At least now Annie might be able to try it and see what was happening inside the house when she couldn't find me outside. If my twin sister could only hear us talking, maybe she'd be able to summon Kathleen in time to get me out of the jam I was in.

Harper led me to the living room and gestured to a straight-backed wooden chair. "Sit down."

"If it's all the same to you, I'd rather be on the couch." I wasn't being fussy about the seating arrangements. The chair would put me out of Annie's line of sight if she peeked in through the door, whereas if I sat on the couch, she'd be able to see me immediately.

"I said the chair," Harper said harshly as she motioned with the blade for me to sit.

"Fine," I said, doing as I was told. I'd already pushed her too far. The conditions weren't ideal, but they were the best I was going to get. "You don't have to hurt me. I really don't know anything."

Harper smiled wryly. "Nice try, but I heard you and your sister talking on the porch a little while ago." The killer looked around, and then she asked, "Where is she, anyway?"

"She's off looking for Franklin," I lied. "See? We still aren't sure who killed Chester."

Harper seemed to buy that, at least for the moment. She moved behind me, and I felt a rope encircle my rib cage, pinning my arms against my sides. Before I knew what was happening, I was trapped in her web. "That's good," she said. "At least one of the leads I gave you paid off. Tell me the truth. I should have just left you alone the entire time, shouldn't I? Did it make you suspicious, how eager I was to provide you with clues about who might have killed Chester?"

"The thought crossed my mind," I admitted. "Why *did* you kill him? Was it because he broke up with you?"

She shook her head. "It was never about love; it was always about the money. Chester changed his will after our second date to include me in it for a minor share. I was going to trick the fool into marrying me so I could get it all, but it didn't work out that way. I saw soon enough that he might be interested in dating me, but marriage was another thing altogether. That's when I decided to cut my losses, get rid of him, collect what I had coming to me, and then go shopping for my next victim."

"Is that when you tried to run him down? It wasn't in your Miata, was it?"

"No, I borrowed my uncle's car, but Chester was too agile for me. When that didn't work, I tried to make it look like a hunting accident, but the fool shot back at me and nearly killed me instead! That's when I got the idea of killing him somewhere in public, where there would be plenty of suspects."

"Why did you choose the Iron, though?" I asked, hoping that Annie was close enough to hear us inside.

"Why not? I saw the pan lying out on the counter the day before, so I thought what better place? It was nothing personal, Pat. You two were convenient, that's all."

I tried not to react, but I wasn't as far out of the line of sight as I'd first suspected. I could see one edge of the door I'd left unlocked slowly begin to open. Was it just Annie, or had she had time to go for reinforcements? Either way, I had to keep Harper talking. "What good is it going to do you killing me, Harper?" I asked.

"You and that twin sister of yours are both too nosy for your own good. After I take care of you, I'm going after her."

"Don't you think Kathleen will figure it out?"

"If I gave her enough time, she probably would, but she won't be alive long enough to come to any conclusions. I'm about to wipe out what's left of the Marsh clan."

From her tone of voice and the look in her eyes, the woman had clearly gone around the bend completely. She was actually under the delusion that she was going to get out of this unscathed.

"Answer something else for me," I said, doing my best to stall her as long as I could. "What made you choose Chester in the first place? From every outward sign, he wasn't a rich man."

"It was purely by accident," she said. "I happened to overhear him talking to Bryson on the phone once, and after I did a little digging on my own, I found out just how much he was really worth. After that, the poor guy didn't stand a chance."

"But then you two had a fight. Help me understand what happened next. You'd already tried to kill him twice, but what was the hurry this time? You could have taken your time and planned something better than hitting him in the back of the head with one of our skillets."

She frowned, clearly angry with herself. "I did something stupid, and he caught me. He threatened to change his will in the morning, so what choice did I have? If I didn't kill him before he spoke with his attorney, all the time that I invested in him would be lost."

"What did you do that was so bad?" I asked, sneaking a glance in Annie's direction.

She was approaching Harper silently from behind, the blade fully extended and pointing toward the killer. Did Annie have what it took to stab Harper in the back? Normally, I would have said no, but with my life hanging in the balance, I had a feeling that she would do anything to save me. I knew that I would have done it without a second thought if the circumstances had been reversed.

"In a moment of weakness, I had a fling with Franklin,"

she admitted. "That was bad enough, but then the fool crowed about it to his younger brother! When that happened, what choice did I have?"

"You could have been loyal to Chester," I said.

She spat on me, a look of hatred on her face. "That's it. I've had enough of you."

I braced myself for the knife attack, preparing to fight back, even if it was futile.

As Harper neared me, there was a crashing sound behind us, and she whirled around to face Annie.

It was just the distraction I needed. Lifting my legs, I kicked out at Harper's back and sent her staggering toward my sister. The kitchen knife flew out of her hands, and I saw her scramble to pick it up, but Annie wasn't going to let her retrieve it that easily. She jumped on the knife herself, her own blade clattering uselessly to the floor. As the women wrestled for the large knife, I knew that I had to act. Pushing myself with everything I had, I managed to shove my chair backward, sending my body crashing to the floor. I'd hoped to loosen the rope, but the outcome was even more spectacular.

The chair split apart upon impact, and I was free.

Better yet, I now had a weapon of my own.

Pushing the rope off me, I grabbed the chair leg that had splintered away and headed for the fray.

I was too late, though.

Harper had won the struggle for the large kitchen knife, and even as I watched, she began to plunge it toward my sister's throat.

CHAPTER 26: ANNIE

I COULDN'T BELIEVE THAT I LOST the battle over the knife with Harper, and too late, I realized that I should have used the small blade Pat had given me instead. I'd panicked, and now I was going to pay for it with my life. Everything seemed to move in slow motion as the blade snaked toward my throat, and though I wanted to squirm away, it was clear that I was out of time.

And then I heard a sound of anger explode from my brother that somehow managed to startle Harper, slowing the blade in her hand for an instant.

I watched as my brother leapt toward us like a man possessed! As Pat landed on her back, he swung the broken chair leg toward the back of her head. Making contact with it, he drove Harper off me and to the floor. I moved quickly out of the way, and this time, I grabbed the knife before Harper could get anywhere near it.

"Call Kathleen," Pat instructed me as he pinned Harper to the floor. There was no way that she could move, let alone threaten either one of us ever again.

I threw the knife into the kitchen and pulled out my cell phone. My hands were shaking so badly that it was difficult to dial Kathleen's number, but I somehow managed it.

Before she could answer, I said breathlessly, "Help. We need you."

Leave it to my sister not to ask me a single question that

wasn't immediately pertinent. "Where are you, and what do you need?"

"We caught Harper. She confessed. We're at her house. Hurry."

I hung up even as my sister was still speaking. I wanted to throw up, but I knew that I had to keep it together long enough for Kathleen to get there. Solving Chester's murder had been more of a puzzle than an actual event, but Harper physically threatening both my brother and me had made it all real enough. We'd been playing for the highest stakes, and despite a pair of very close calls, we'd lived to see the end of it.

That didn't mean that I ever wanted to do it again, though.

I leaned down toward Pat, who was still fighting to keep Harper down. "Are you okay?"

"I'm going to be sore tomorrow from hitting the floor, but I'll live," he said. "Stop moving!" he commanded, but Harper continued to struggle.

"Should I hit her with the chair leg, too?" I offered in a rational voice. It seemed like a perfectly reasonable offer and one I never thought I'd ever have to make.

Harper quit fighting the moment I made the suggestion.

"She's okay now," Pat said. That's when I noticed some blood on the back of his head seeping down his neck.

"How about you? You're bleeding. Did she cut you?"

"No, I must have scraped it when I broke the chair," he said with a grin. "With the adrenaline rushing through my system, I don't feel a thing."

"I've got a hunch that you will soon enough," I said.

A moment later, I heard the sirens.

Kathleen was on her way.

I didn't really breathe again until Harper was handcuffed. She'd gotten her second wind and was struggling mightily and cursing everyone in sight as they led her out to the squad car. We caught

Kathleen up to date, and she offered to give us a ride to the hospital so a doctor could take a look at Pat's injury.

"Thanks, but if you don't mind, I'd rather drive him myself," I volunteered. "I appreciate you not lecturing us about what we did."

Our sister shrugged. "That will come later, after I'm sure that you're both okay. Seriously, though, you two took a real chance coming here and facing her alone."

"You were sure it was Franklin, remember?" I asked her with a grin.

"Don't remind me," she said. "I'll catch up with you later." She started to go, and then, on the spur of the moment, our sister the sheriff decided that neither one of us was going to get out of there without being hugged.

I couldn't speak for Pat, but it was certainly welcome for me.

———— ❧ ————

As I drove him to the hospital, Pat said, "I didn't think you'd ever show up."

"I was there longer than you might think. I kept waiting for her to make a mistake, but when she didn't, I decided to come in and force the issue myself."

"I thought you might call for reinforcements," Pat said.

"If I took the time to do that, you might not have made it." The realization of how close I'd come to losing my twin brother was just about more than I could stand.

"That's true," he said. "Thanks for saving me, by the way."

"Are you kidding? I would be dead if it hadn't been for your attack. What was with that scream, by the way? I knew it was you, and it still sent chills through me."

He smiled slightly and then winced a little as he started feeling the pain from his impact. "It was my war cry."

"Well, whatever it was, it worked."

As I drove, I kept glancing over at my brother. He had been right before; he'd saved my life, but I'd saved his as well. I tried to never take him for granted, but after what we'd just been through together, I was going to make it a point to make sure that he knew how much I loved him each and every day. It wouldn't hurt to tell our big sister Kathleen that, as well.

My family might not have been perfect, but it was plenty good enough for me.

CHAPTER 27: PAT

T HE NEXT DAY, THINGS WERE pretty much back to normal, if there ever was such a thing. I had a small bandage on the back of my neck where a splintered piece of chair had scraped it, and I felt as though I'd been beaten up by seven angry men, but nothing was broken, and I knew that given a little time, I'd be good as new. Annie and I were both at the Iron, exactly where we belonged. Edith was distributing the day's mail to all of the tiny boxes, Skip was dusting the wares on his shelf, Annie was working the breakfast grill, and I was at the register.

A man I vaguely recognized came in with a serious frown on his face. "You're Pat, aren't you?"

"I am. Do I know you?"

"We met once a long time ago. I'm Greg Daily, Molly's cousin from Charlotte."

I knew I'd heard that voice before. "You were at her place the other night, weren't you?"

"That was me," he admitted. "To tell you the truth, that's what I wanted to talk to you about. Listen, Molly would kill me if she knew that I were here, but I'm on my way out of town, and there's something I have to tell you before I go. Don't give up on her, okay?"

"What? She was pretty clear about where things stood."

He nodded, accompanying the movement with a frown. "She made a mistake, and she knows it. I don't know what it's going to take for you two to work things out, but life's too short not to be happy, you know what I mean?" He looked around the Iron and smiled. "This is a nice place you have here."

"Thanks. We like it."

"Remember, this is just between the two of us. See you around, Pat."

"Bye," I said, wondering if what Greg had just told me was really true. Was Molly having second thoughts about giving up on us? If there was the slightest chance of us ever getting back together, I was going to do whatever it took to make it happen. I'd come too close to dying, and it had taught me one thing more than any other: life was for the living. I wanted to be the happiest that I could manage, and if that meant that I had to make a fool out of myself pursuing the love of my life, then so be it.

Today was indeed a new day, and I meant to take full advantage of it.

RECIPES

CAST IRON BEEF STEW

We like to have this meal when it's cold outside, but honestly, it's good any time of year. This stew, as with many of the cast iron dishes we enjoy, can be cooked outside over a campfire just as easily as on the stovetop or in the oven inside. There's something about the heartiness of this offering that appeals to me and my family, and the aromas that waft through the house are almost worth the trouble to make this meal even if you didn't have such a delightful ending waiting for you when you dished out the food!

Ingredients

- Beef stew meat, 1.5 to 2 pounds, browned
- 1/4 cup all-purpose flour
- 4 to 5 carrots, cut into substantial wedges
- 1 teaspoon olive oil
- 1 onion, large and cut into wedges as well
- 4 potatoes, quartered if russet, whole if red
- Beef or vegetable broth, 14.5 oz. (1 can)
- Tap water 14.5 oz. (use the broth container to measure)
- 2 teaspoons table salt
- 2 teaspoons crushed pepper
- 2 bay leaves

- A dash of dried thyme

Optional

- 1/4 cup cornstarch mixed into a slurry with 1/4 cup lukewarm water if a heartier sauce is desired

Directions

Preheat your oven to 300°F.

Next, coat the beef chunks in flour, and then brown them in your cast iron Dutch oven using olive oil over medium heat. Add the carrots, onions, potatoes, broth, water, salt, pepper, bay leaves, and dried thyme, then stir to mix. Add the cornstarch slurry if a heartier liquid is desired. Cover and bake three to four hours, or until the meat, potatoes, and carrots are fork tender. Remove the bay leaves and serve.

Serves 4 to 6 hearty appetites

Note: This meal goes extremely well with the cornbread recipe listed below.

CORNBREAD

I grew up eating brown beans and cornbread, a staple that I still enjoy to this day. I have to say, though, this particular recipe has evolved quite a bit over time. What started off as a basic mix has since developed into a star addition to just about any meal. The jalapenos are optional, but I highly recommend them! If you find they are too spicy, just reduce the amount used the next time you make it. As far as I'm concerned, it lacks a little something when you omit them altogether.

Ingredients

- 2 tablespoons butter (we used salted, but unsalted is fine as well)
- 1/4 cup onion, diced
- 1/2 green bell pepper, diced
- 1/2 cup corn kernels, frozen
- 1 tablespoon jalapenos, diced (jarred work fine, or fresh will do as well)
- 1 box or bag cornbread mix (approx. 7.5 oz.)
- 1/2 cup buttermilk (I used to use fresh, but I've recently switched to the powdered and can't tell any difference)
- 1 egg, beaten
- 1/2 cup shredded cheese (I like sharp or extra-sharp cheddar, but you can use just about any kind you like)
- 1 tablespoon oil (I use olive oil in my cast iron to both cook and season the pans)

Directions

In a cast iron skillet (10-inch for tall cornbread, 12-inch for flatter, crisper bread), melt the butter under medium heat, and then cook the onion and pepper until the onion is almost translucent. Next, add the frozen corn and the diced jalapenos, stirring until the corn is thawed. Take this off the heat and set aside. Next, in a medium-sized bowl, empty the cornbread mix, and then add the buttermilk and the beaten egg, mixing until mostly incorporated. Add the veggies (and jalapenos if desired), and finally put in the shredded cheese, mixing again until nearly incorporated into the mix as well. Add the olive oil to the cast iron skillet and heat until warm. Pour the batter in, and then bake from 20 to 30 minutes at 375°F, or until the top begins to brown and the edges pull away from the sides. Remove, cut into wedges, and serve. We like to have some real butter nearby, as it is pure ambrosia when it melts into the cornbread. It is truly delightful!

Serves 3 to 6, depending on the size of your slices

If you enjoy Jessica Beck mysteries and you would like to be notified when the next book is being released, please send your email address to **newreleases@jessicabeckmysteries.net**. Your email address will not be shared, sold, bartered, traded, broadcast, or disclosed in any way. There will be no spam from us, just a friendly reminder when the latest book is being released.

Also, be sure to visit our website at jessicabeckmysteries.net for valuable information about Jessica's books.

OTHER BOOKS BY JESSICA BECK

Made in the USA
San Bernardino, CA
27 January 2016